THE FIRST VICTIM

When he got home from work that day, John Braun felt a little funny. It seemed as if he were breaking out all over in a rash that itched badly. But he couldn't see anything on his skin and so, dead tired, he undressed and went to bed.

He woke up in what seemed minutes. And now there was no doubt that something was wrong. He could barely breathe. Besides, here was an indescribable, blanketed feeling to all his body. He called a doctor and gasped out his plea for help.

John Braun was unconscious when the doctor arrived. After one look at Braun ,the doctor called the police. For Braun's body looked as if someone had sifted powdered sugar all over him. The stuff was dust-fine, and glittered softy with an almost crystalline appearance.

"Gosh!" whispered the detective. "The guy looks like a snow man!"

A snow man. And the first victim of The Frosted Death.

Also In This Series

By Kenneth Robeson

AVENGER #1: JUSTICE INC.

AVENGER #2: THE YELLOW HOARD

AVENGER #3: THE SKY WALKER

AVENGER #4: THE DEVIL'S HORNS

THE FROSTED DEATH

by Kenneth Robeson

PAPERBACK LIBRARY
NEW YORK

WARNER PAPERBACK LIBRARY EDITION

First Printing: October, 1972

This Warner Paperback Library Edition is published by arrangement with The Condé Nast Publications, Inc.

Warner Paperback Library is a division of Warner Books, Inc., 315 Park Avenue South, New York, N.Y. 10010.

CHAPTER I

The Glass Capsule

The man was a perfect example of the way in which fate sometimes selects obscure persons for great historic roles.

He was certainly obscure enough. His name was John Braun, pronounced Brown. He was average in height, average in weight, average in brain power, and average in earning capacity. Mr. John Q. Public, himself. Yet fate chose him as the first one.

Braun worked on the night shift at the Laddex Rubber Co. on lower Eighth Avenue, New York City. He earned twenty-four dollars and eighty cents a week, on which he supported a wife and sister. The wife and sister were away at the time—which was very lucky, indeed, for the wife and sister.

Because the great role fate had selected for John Braun was that of victim; and if the two women had been at home with him they would have been victims, too.

The night was fairly warm. Braun was walking the mile to his apartment, instead of taking the subway. He walked with carefree stride, swinging his black tin lunchbox.

Now and then he looked dreamily at the sky. It was clear, and the night was filled with stars. It reminded

Braun of the farm from which he had come, eighteen years before, to take a city job.

He was looking up, in the shadow of a building taller than the rest around here, when it happened. But he didn't see it fall.

The first thing of which he was aware, was a swift little *swish* as something fell past his ear. Then there was a shrill small sound, as something smashed to a million fragments at his feet. After that—nothing.

Thus, simply, did fate usher Braun into posterity.

Braun looked up again. The building from which this thing apparently had fallen was nineteen stories high. It was all dark, save for the top floor. Presumably the thing had fallen from there.

But what was it that had fallen?

Braun stopped. Covering the sidewalk for ten feet around were bits of glass so small that they looked pulverized. The thing that had fallen had been a glass bottle, or vial, or capsule.

He looked around to see what had been in the capsule, to see if it had smashed, too. But there seemed to have been nothing at all in it. There weren't even traces of moisture on the sidewalk to indicate a liquid of some sort.

Braun decided the little glass container had been empty. In which case its fall meant nothing. There was nothing to return to the lighted top-floor space from which it had toppled; nothing to be done but go on home and be thankful that the little glass thing hadn't hit him on the head. From that height, even a small object, dropped squarely on you, would give you something more than a headache!

He walked on toward his dingy apartment, swinging his black lunchbox.

In the lighted top floor of the nineteen-story building, there was plenty of activity after the fall of the glass capsule.

The building was the Sangaman-Veshnir Building, which housed the main offices of the gigantic Sangaman-Veshnir Drug Corp. On the seventeenth and eighteenth floors were row after row of general offices. On the nineteenth floor was the experimental laboratory and the big offices belonging to the partners, Sangaman and Veshnir.

It was from the laboratory that the glass capsule had dropped. There was a window open next to a workbench and the bench was a little higher than the sill. An object rolling off the bench would be quite apt to roll onto the sill and bounce on out into thin air—which was what the capsule had done.

In the laboratory were two men. One was a fellow named Targill, brilliant graduate of a well-known school of scientific research. The other was Carl Veshnir. The faces of both were distorted with frenzied emotion. But the expressions were different.

Veshnir's emotion was an almost insane anger and nothing else. Targill's was a blend of contrition, fear, and sheer horror.

"If this entire building had fallen, crushing every soul in its path," Targill gasped, "it would have been less terrible than for the capsule to fall from that window! We must repair the damage at once."

Veshnir faced him, snarling. Veshnir was fifty-four, stout, florid-faced, and normally a very benevolent-looking person. He looked, indeed, like a deacon in a church.

But not now!

"What do you mean—repair the damage?"

Targill, tall and stooped and scholarly appearing, said stubbornly:

"We must act before that horror spreads in the city. Get it under control. We must call the police and have them rush a squad car. Quarantine anyone who may have happened to be passing nearby when the thing fell. Rope off the area under the window."

"Are you insane?" snarled Veshnir. "You know what it would mean if the nature of this experiment, and our connection with it, became known. And it certainly would become known if we communicated with the police!"

"Everything's off now," Targill said desperately. "Nothing matters now. Only the thing that dropped. Phone the police."

"No!"

"You realize what might happen to New York if you don't—"

"I won't phone the police!"

"Then I will!"

"No!"

Veshnir got between the laboratory telephone and the frantic head-chemist for Sangaman-Veshnir Drug Corp.

"Man! Every second counts!"

Veshnir stood where he was. Targill took several steps toward him, then stopped. Veshnir was a bigger man than he. The chemist began pacing frantically up and down the lab, beating the back of his fist against his forehead.

The laboratory was a curious room. All the apparatus in it, normally in use for a dozen experiments, had been shoved aside out of the way of a great table and several benches on which only one experiment was taking the limelight.

On the table and workbenches were many flat, shallow pans, with glass lids carefully fitted over them. In the pans were snow.

At least it looked like snow—fine, white snow.

On the big table, among the pans, lay a small, dead piglet. The little porker had been shaved, as if in preparation for a barbecue. Every part of its hide had been shaved clean. And it wore pants. A small pair of trousers, made from a thick towel, swathed porcine waist and hams.

Targill stared at the pig in pants with eyes literally glazed with terror, as if the dead piglet were some frightful monster about to spring at him.

"I tell you, we've got to phone headquarters about what happened!" he croaked. "Are you a human being, that you can ignore a thing like that? There are seven and a half million helpless souls in this vicinity—"

"I'm human enough," snapped Veshnir. "Human enough to want my share of the biggest thing that's ever happened under this roof. You'll get a huge share, too."

"I don't want a share at such a price. I've done a lot of things that weren't quite straight. I'd do them again. I'm no saint. But this—oh, no!"

Targill started toward the phone with his fists clenched. Veshnir grabbed up a small lead case in which was a radium needle.

"Stand aside, Veshnir!"

Veshnir stood where he was, teeth showing between parted lips.

"My friend," he said softly, "it is better to be a live—and rich—man of discretion, than a dead hero."

"You wouldn't dare," whispered Targill.

Veshnir continued to smile, teeth naked and ugly, like the fangs of an animal.

"You wouldn't dare," Targill repeated.

And he leaped for the older man.

On the table, the dead pig in its grotesque pants, seemed to stare as if with grim approval.

CHAPTER II

Page The Avenger

There were lights on the top floor of the Sangaman-Veshnir Building other than those in the laboratory. There were lights in Thomas Sangaman's big private office, too.

Sangaman was the elder partner. He was over sixty, and he didn't look well. There were lines in his thin, sensitive face. His gray hair was thinning at the forehead. His hands trembled a little at their task.

The task was the examination of the company books for the last six months. The books told a very disquieting story.

The Sangaman-Veshnir Drug Corp. was a big one. It was a twenty-million-dollar outfit. It had branches all over the country and a few in Europe. But its size wasn't doing much for it at the moment.

The company was in a very bad way, financially.

From time to time Sangaman turned a page of neat figures, frowning at their import. From time to time he absently poured and drank black coffee out of a thermos bottle on his desk. It was well after midnight, but he hadn't a thought of going home, yet. He had to finish his examination of the books and learn the whole story of disaster.

What it amounted to was that the corporation was bankrupt, right this minute. It would be public news inside of a week.

Most of the trouble was Veshnir. Sangaman had always known that; but he hadn't realized till now just how *much* of it was Veshnir's doing.

The complete story of failure lay in the fact that Veshnir just naturally seemed to be a born chiseler. The man couldn't do things in an open, aboveboard fashion. He seemed to prefer to make a dollar in a deal that was slightly shady rather than twenty dollars in a decent business transaction.

Sangaman had known of his partner's tendency to chisel since the early days. He had found it out in a few months after their partnership had been formed. But he had put up with it. The business was growing rapidly in spite of Veshnir. The public had accepted them as a pair, and Sangaman hated to break it up. Besides, Veshnir had ability as a sales executive, and once or twice by his close dealing had pulled the firm out of a bad hole.

So Sangaman went along with him, and played his tendencies down, and kept him as straight as he could. Sangaman's own reputation was so honorable that it kept Veshnir's whitewashed. In addition to which, Veshnir's look of being a benevolent deacon helped get him by.

But in the last year, the books showed, something seemed to have happened to Veshnir. He had become worse. There were transactions in which the corporation had taken terrific losses because Veshnir tried to shave the law too fine. There was a deal or two creating the suspicion that money had been made—but had gone into Veshnir's private account instead of into the firm's treasury.

The office door opened and Veshnir came in. Sangaman looked at him inscrutably, not yet quite ready to confront his partner with his suspicions and, at last, have it out. Veshnir, he thought, looked a little pale and agitated.

"About through?" Veshnir asked Sangaman, sitting on Sangaman's desk with his back to the coffee thermos.

"Oh, no," said Sangaman evenly. "I'll be here for another hour, anyway."

"I should think you'd leave the books to an accountant instead of going over them yourself," said Veshnir, taking a cigar from his vest. He fumbled for a match, did not find one, and reached behind him for a lighter—which was near the thermos.

"It looks to me," said Sangaman, watching him light the cigar, "as if it would be best to keep the books away from accountants, right now."

"Is that so?"

"I don't have to tell you, do I?"

"I guess things aren't too good," Veshnir said vaguely.

"That's a mild way to put it!"

"Oh, well," said Veshnir, getting up. "We can probably get old August Taylor to come through with some more capital. What's he a silent partner for, if not to put up money when we need it?"

He went back to the door.

"More laboratory work?" Sangaman said.

Veshnir nodded.

"What in the world are you and Targill doing in there evey night?"

"Working on an experiment."

"So I gathered," Sangaman said dryly. Then: "I don't like Targill."

"What's wrong with him?"

"He's too—ruthless. It isn't right for a man, with as much power to harm as an expert chemist has, to be as shifty as Targill."

"You'd be surprised," said Veshnir, biting down on his cigar, "how kindly Targill can be. Well, duck in and say good night when you leave."

Sangaman nodded; then he turned back to the books when Veshnir left.

It was on the next to the last page that he saw something that riveted his attention even more than the rest. It was an item concerning a foreign country; one that is in a constant state of military preparedness amounting almost to actual warfare.

There was no story to be drawn from the item. It wasn't complete enough, and it did not occur again. The product listed was simple enough: crude drugs.

The only trouble being that the Sangaman-Veshnir Drug Corp. did not sell crude drugs to that particular country.

Sangaman gulped black coffee and thought hard.

There was a mystery here that needed solving. And that brought to his mind, like a light in a dark place, one name—that of a man who made mystery his business.

Richard Henry Benson, known as The Avenger.

Sangaman reached for the phone.

Sangaman dialed a number, and a mile or so away, a telephone rang.

It rang in a curious place, on Bleek Street. Bleek Street is only a short block long. On one side is the back end of a concrete storage warehouse, taking up a whole block. The building shuts off that side like a great wall. On the other side are several stores and, in the center, three old brick buildings.

The three buildings, owned by Benson, were thrown together into one and used as his headquarters. The other places were rented by him on long lease. In effect, he owned the block.

The telephone, dialed by Sangaman, rang in a tremendous room taking up the whole top of the three buildings. He heard a girl's voice answer, then said:

"I would like to speak to Mr. Benson, please."

The voice, low and sweet, replied politely: "I am sorry. Mr. Benson has just left. Is there a message?"

Sangaman thought a moment, then said, disappointedly: "No—I'll call later."

He hung up. And in the Bleek Street room a lovely

small blonde traced the call as a matter of routine, determining that it came from one of the private lines of the Sangaman-Veshnir Drug Corp.

In his office, Sangaman got up and started toward the door. He meant to ask Veshnir about that one obscure item concerning the warlike foreign power. But he didn't reach the door. Something seemed to hit him on the head, and he sagged to his knees.

He looked dazedly around. There was no one in the office but himself: so it could not have been a physical blow. He tried hazily to get up, and saw the floor seeming to rush upward to hit him.

Richard Henry Benson, The Avenger, had just stepped out, as the pretty blond girl had said. He had gone out because just before Sangaman called for help, the police had called for the same reason. The police had learned what The Avenger could do; so every once in a while, now, they paged The Avenger and asked for assistance.

The help they wanted, this time, concerned a little-known worker in the Laddex Rubber Co. named John Braun.

Braun had gotten home about ten minutes after the queer glass capsule burst at his feet. He had felt a little funny on entering his apartment. It was a peculiar sensation. It seemed as if he were breaking out all over in a rash that itched badly. But he couldn't see anything on his skin.

The itching subsided a little, so he undressed quickly and went to bed. The apartment seemed dreary and empty with his wife and sister away on a visit. He was glad to fall asleep as quickly as a tired man, after a hard eight hours' work, does.

He woke up in what seemed a few minutes. And now there was no doubt at all about there being something wrong with him. It was dark; so he couldn't see himself. And that was just as well for had he looked at his body, he might have lost his reason.

John Braun could hardly breathe. He felt as if he were choking to death. And so he was, if he had only known it. Besides, there was an indescribable, blanketed feeling to all his body. When he'd been a kid, the small school he'd attended had given a play. A foolish teacher had gilded the upper half of his body for the part he had to play. There had been a lot of trouble till the local doctor could get the stuff off so that his skin could breathe again.

He felt now, all over his body, as he had felt then, from the waist up.

The phone was on a stand beside his bed. He reached for it, in darkness. He didn't know if he would be able to get up and walk to the light.

He called a doctor and gasped out his plea for help. He was too weak, by then, to hang up the receiver. The phone dropped from his lax hand, as he sagged back in bed.

The doctor came in a hurry. And after one look, he called the police in even more of a hurry.

It was the investigating detective who, glancing at the unconscious man in bed, had gotten in touch with The Avenger.

John Braun, lying naked on the bed with the covers turned back for medical examination, looked as if someone had sifted powdered sugar all over him. The stuff was dust-fine, and glittered softly with an almost crystalline appearance.

"Gosh!" whispered the detective. "The guy looks like a snow man!"

The comparison was apt. Braun lay in the bed like a figure of fine, dazzling white snow. Only he didn't melt as a snow man would have in the warm room.

CHAPTER III

The Snow Man

The fact that Braun's bedroom was so small and dark and bare brought out the terror of the thing all the more sharply.

Braun's body seemed to concentrate the dim light from the simple bulb within itself, and to glow as if with an inner fire. It was like a snow figure with a small searchlight on it. You felt dazzled when you looked at it.

The doctor was feeling around with a puzzled hand. He scraped some of the whitish, powdery stuff from a bit of Braun's dead arm. The skin was exposed for only a few seconds. Then it filmed over again. The skin seemed to cloud, as a mirror does when you breathe on it; then it soon presented that powdered-sugar look again.

"It's a kind of growth!" the doctor said, shocked. "A sort of fungus, I'd say, almost microscopically fine. Though it looks almost like an inert mineral substance."

"You mean the guy is moldy?" asked the detective, with no intention whatever of being funny.

"Yes. In a way, the stuff is like mold. Only I have never seen anything spread so fast. It reproduces itself, literally, while you watch it."

The detective shivered, and drew a sheet over the dead

face. The eyes were open, and the powdered-sugar substance had reached them by now. The eyeballs looked like snow-covered ice.

"Is it some new kind of disease, or what?" asked the detective.

"I don't know," the doctor replied. "I suppose that's as close as we can name it, right now."

"Then it isn't a case for the homicide squad," the detective said, relieved.

"I wouldn't be too sure of that." The doctor absently scratched at his hand. "This may have been caused, not by nature, but some human brain, somehow. I wonder where the fungi originated, and how?"

In the place where the powdery, glittering stuff had originated, the Sangaman-Veshnir laboratory, Veshnir stood near the lab door with his head bent in a strained, listening attitude. He was listening for sounds in the adjoining chamber—Sangaman's office.

At Veshnir's feet was a figure already beginning to stiffen a little. It was Targill's body! The whole top of the chief chemist's head was knocked in. The weapon that had done it lay next to the corpse. It was the oblong lead case in which was the radium needle.

While Veshnir listened in the direction of Sangaman's office, he stared at the corpse near his feet. And in his eyes was a horrible fear.

"I had to do it!" he muttered, staring at the body. "The fool would have told the police all about it. It was his fault, not mine. I had to do it!"

But having to commit a murder, and getting away with it, are two different things.

There were on the top floor of the building, and had been ever since ten o'clock that night, only three people. Those three, only souls in the place save for the building watchman and the assistant engineer in the basement, were on record as being present. When you went into the building after hours, no matter who you were, you were required to sign a register in the lobby. Then the watchman ran you up to whatever floor you called.

So it was a matter of inescapable record that only Targill, Veshnir and Sangaman were up there. No one else had come in.

Now Targill was dead! And automatically it became iron-clad fact that only one of the remaining two could be the murderer.

Either Veshnir or Sangaman was going to face the chair.

"But I had to do it," Veshnir whispered again. "There are millions, scores of millions, in it if it can be kept secret. But there isn't a cent in it if it gets publicity—as it would have if Targill phoned the cops."

So Targill had had to die. But now—

There was a sound from Sangaman's office. A curiously unsteady step, then a thump, and after that the solid thud of a body as Sangaman fell near the door in his curious dizzy spell.

Veshnir drew a great sigh of pure relief.

"It's all right, now," he said aloud. "Everything's all right now."

Sangaman slowly swam back to consciousness. His senses cleared so that he began to be aware of things around him. But one of the first things of which he was aware was a queer feeling—more of a hunch than anything else—that he had been *half* conscious for quite a few minutes. He had faint recollections of moving around, of having something in his hand. Some metal. It was as if his conscious brain had been cut off, but his body seemed to have been able to roam around and do—Heaven knew what.

He looked around. He was in the laboratory. He remembered he had started to come out here when the odd seizure downed him. He had intended to confront Veshnir—

Veshnir was here, standing right in front of him—and looking down at him with an accusing expression that was most perplexing.

"Why," asked Veshnir, voice incredulous, "did you do it?"

"Do what?" said Sangaman. It seemed to him that his voice came from a distance.

"Kill him?"

"Kill *who?*" said Sangaman, blinking.

He tried to get to his knees, but he couldn't make it, yet. He sat there, body swaying. He must have been working too hard over those books.

"You know who! I got to the hall door just in time to see you strike him down."

Sangaman discovered that one reason why he wasn't able to get up was that there was something in his right hand that slid along the floor when he tried to brace himself. He looked down stupidly at it. It was the lead case containing the radium needle. There was blood on the sharp corner of the heavy little casket.

Then Sangaman looked farther—and gasped. There was a hand and arm trailing along the floor like dead seaweed. The arm was in a white laboratory coat sleeve. He looked on past the shoulder.

"Targill!"

"Yes. Dead!" said Veshnir. "You mean to say you didn't remember? A thing like *that?"*

Veshnir repeated his story.

"I was at the laboratory washroom, just off the hall. I came back, opened the door and saw you facing Targill. You had your right hand raised. The lead case was in it. I opened the door just as you brought it down on his head. Then you seemed to faint or something."

"I killed Targill? You're mad!"

"You must remember some of it," Veshnir said.

Sangaman's face screwed up in the most intensive thinking of his life. The devil of it was that he *did* remember a little. A very little. Enough to be sure that he had moved around some during his lapse of memory and voluntary action—though he couldn't recall what he had done.

Sweat began to break out on his forehead. Gone forever

was the thought of finances and books that had brought him in here. There was only room for the one terrible thing.

"I didn't hit him, Veshnir!" he pleaded. "I swear it! I'd know if I—"

"Of course that would be your story," nodded Veshnir. "And I'll stand by you through thick and thin. I'll swear, too, that you were nowhere near the laboratory when Targill died. However—"

Sangaman hung on his words, his look.

"Well? Well?" he croaked.

"There isn't, really, much chance to lie out of it. There are only the two of us here—with a dead man. And your prints are on that lead case, along with his blood."

"Veshnir, on the memory of your mother, as you hope for deliverance when you die—did I do what you said you saw me do?"

"I'm sorry," said Veshnir, with infinite pity on his benevolent countenance, "you did. I think I begin to see why. You'd worked too hard over those books. You got up and came into the laboratory to see me. You saw Targill instead. You have always hated him—said he was ruthless and shifty. Now, you were in a sort of coma. You felt the lead case under your hand, and not knowing in the least what you were doing, you killed him with it. Then you fainted, coming to about five minutes later."

Sangaman shuddered. If only one small thing hadn't happened, he wouldn't believe this impossible thing for a second. But the one thing shook him. That was the fact that he had come to with the definite impression on his mind that he had been moving around, subconsciously, a short time *before* that.

"I don't care! I won't believe it!"

"I'm afraid the police will believe it," Veshnir said. "See the facts. Only the three of us are here. One of us must have murdered Targill. But it is well known that he and I worked together, were on fine terms, and that his death brings to a premature close an important piece of laboratory work. It is equally well known, on the other hand, that you disliked him very much and would have fired him if I hadn't intervened."

Sangaman moaned and rubbed his splitting head.

"I still won't believe I really did such a thing, conscious or unconscious! But—what shall I do?"

Veshnir shook his head.

"I don't know. I will support any statement you choose to make, as I said. But I'm afraid—no statement will do any good."

"Veshnir—*you* were in here alone with Targill."

"Naturally," Veshnir said quietly, "you would think of that. Everyone will. But not for long. As I pointed out, I was working with him on a very important experiment. There might have been millions in it. His death is a great loss to me—but not to you."

Sangaman was on his feet, now, swaying. He felt the lead case in his hand and dropped it as if it had burned his fingers.

"What shall I do? Oh, what shall I do?"

Veshnir was looking very thoughtful.

"I'm afraid you haven't a chance if you get picked up, now. But later, after we've gotten together the best battery of legal talent procurable, you may. Or perhaps we can get together some prominent psychiatrists who could prove you did it in a temporary fit of insanity."

"So?" said Sangaman pleadingly. He was stunned, dazed, unable to think.

"If you're caught now, everything is lost. If we have time, there may be hope. It's everything to gain and nothing to lose. I'd advise you to hide somewhere for a while."

"Where in the world could I hide? The call will be out for me the minute this is found out. I couldn't go home—or anywhere else."

"I don't know where—" Veshnir began. Then he stopped abruptly. "But, yes! I do know. Last fall I picked up a new summer place in Maine. North of Bangor. It's a rough place—for shooting and camping. There's a log cabin, nearly a thousand acres of woods, not a soul on it. It isn't even known that it's in my name. I bought it secretly. You can go there."

Sangaman was in a fog. It was impossible that he had done murder, even in a moment of mental disorder. But—there the body was! And the whole police force would be sure he was the killer, and would pin it on him in an hour's investigation.

Brokenly he accepted Veshnir's proposition.

"Wipe my prints off that case," he said, at the door.

"Of course!" Veshnir said.

But as the door closed, he did not wipe the case. He placed it a little closer to the dead chemist's head, handling it with a handkerchief around his fingers to keep his own prints off.

CHAPTER IV

Death's Myriad Touch

All over the country the various police forces were getting more and more familiar with the work of Richard Henry Benson, The Avenger. There wasn't a police chief in the United Sttaes who didn't know of him.

But here in New York, where The Avenger had his headquarters, every cop on the force knew about him, from the greenest rookie up. That was why the homicide man had called Benson, without question, a few minutes after looking at the corpse that was so eerily like a snow man.

The doctor was curious. He, like most ordinary citizens, didn't know about Benson.

"How is it," he said, "that the police department calls on a private citizen like this? Or is Benson with the Federal law department?"

"No, he's a private citizen," said the detective.

"But I don't—"

The homicide man looked around mechanically to see if any reporters were in earshot. Because if there were, he'd have had to soft-pedal about The Avenger. Not only did the force dislike to go on record as asking help outside itself, but also, Benson hated publicity.

"He's a private citizen," the detective said, "but not like any other private citizen you ever saw. He's an average-sized guy, but he can throw any man on the force. And we got some upward of six feet six and weighing two hundred and fifty. He has pure white hair, but still he's young. Got it overnight in a nerve shock when his wife and kid were taken away by gangsters. His face was paralyzed at the same time, so he's always dead pan. Gives you the heebies to look at him. His eyes give you the willies, too. They're light gray. Anyhow, I guess they're gray: they're so light they look almost like colorless holes in his face. He's something, that guy!"

"But surely he doesn't have only a peculiar physical appearance to make him so important?" queried the doctor, one eyebrow up.

"I'll say not! He's got *everything* on the ball. The guy is a whiz at science in all its branches. He's a genius at sniffing out crime where no one else can smell it. He has a laboratory that's twice as good as the big one down in Washington. He—"

A tap at the door interrupted him.

"That'll be him," he said, starting toward the door.

"So soon?" said the doctor. "Why, he couldn't get here this fast—"

"There are no speed laws for *him,*" said the homicide man. "And no red lights—Hello, Mr. Benson. Thanks a lot for coming around."

The man who stepped into the dark, shabby little room which cupped a dead, white body as a cellar might cup a snow figure, justified everything the detective had said about him. The doctor got that at a glance.

A white, awesome, moveless face turned toward the corpse, then turned around the room to take photographic-mind pictures of it. Colorless eyes, flaming like ice under a polar dawn, came to rest on the physician's face. The doctor felt something like a physical shock, as if the end of a live wire had brushed him.

The Avenger had no store of small talk. Quiet, invariably polite, he was yet as blunt and direct as a machine. And, figuratively, he was a machine. Crime had ruined his life. It had taken from him the lovely wife and the small daughter from whom he had drawn all his inspiration for living. At the same time it had made him into a machine to fight similar crime.

He nodded in acknowledgement of the doctor's self-introduction and raked the detective with his colorless, terrible eyes.

"Name of the man?" he asked.

"John Braun. No record in police files as far as I know, Mr. Benson."

"We'll check that later. Occupation?"

"He works in a rubber-goods factory—the Laddex Co., up on Eighth Avenue."

"Trouble?" said The Avenger, eyes turning to the doctor.

The doctor cleared his throat. They were uncanny, those eyes. They made you feel as if they read everything you thought. He knew that in a few seconds, fight against it as he might, they could have hypnotized him.

"The trouble," he said respectfully, "is a most obscure one. In fact it's utterly beyond me—unlike anything I have ever seen. The man's epidermis seems to have been attacked by some swift-growing fungus. On the order, perhaps, of saccharomyces. If you understand the scientific term."

The detective snorted. "Look, doc, this guy knows everything. You don't have to pull your punches."

The Avenger, top-ranking physician himself, though he did not practice, said quietly:

"Hardly everything. But I know a little about saccharomyces. A glance at the body would seem to disprove your idea, doctor. Saccharomyces is yellowish. This stuff is dead-white."

"It's only a guess," shrugged the doctor. "It neither looks nor acts like saccharomyces, but—"

"What," said the detective plaintively, "is this here saccharomyces?"

"Yeast," said The Avenger.

He went to the bed, and bent low over the body to study it. But it was noticeable that he didn't touch the corpse.

His colorless, awe-inspiring eyes studied the dead-white, softly glistening thing that looked like a snow man. So white, so ghastly with its seeming inner light. As dead-white as—as The Avenger's dead-white hair.

"I've never seen anything like this," he said in a low tone. And for a person who had seen about everything on earth there was to see, that was an admission.

"You know nothing of how the man may have picked it up? Nothing of his previous movements?"

The doctor shook his head.

"Braun was unconscious when I got here. I had to get the janitor to open the door for me. He was dead when this detective from the homicide squad arrived."

"What did you learn from his employers, the Laddex people?" The Avenger asked the detective.

"They say Braun was all right when he left the shop at midnight, after his four-to-twelve shift. I talked to his foreman."

"Then something happened between the time he left the shop and the time he arrived home."

The detective ventured to disagree.

"Maybe it's something occupational. Rubber shops have funny chemicals, and stuff. I'm going to check on that."

Benson nodded, and his colorless eyes raked the snow man again. He took a comb from the dresser, and with the back of it, carefully scraped some of the dreadful, white, powdery stuff from the dead man's skin. He watched the area closely.

It did as it had done when the doctor performed a similar experiment: the skin was clear for half a minute, then it began to fog over as a mirror does when breathed on. It was as if an unseen hand were sifting fine, powdered sugar over the area. In about two and a half minutes, the cleared section of skin was clear no longer. It was as powdered, as frozen and snowy-looking as the rest.

"It's . . . rather terrible, isn't it?" breathed the doctor.

"It's all of that." The Avenger's head, with its virile shock of pure-white hair, nodded agreement. "I would suggest that you wash in your strongest disinfectant, doctor, if you have touched this man."

"I already have."

"Do it again," said Benson. "And allow no one else to touch the body, under any circumstances."

"You think this is—contagious?"

"I have an idea it is. Though we won't know without exhaustive experiments. Take no chances anyway."

The Avenger went to the dingy kitchen of the small apartment. He came back with a Mason jar. The jar had had preserves in it. He had emptied it and washed it clean with boiling water.

Carefully he scooped some of the stuff that looked like powdered sugar—but that was dreadfully, incredibly alive—from the dead man's chest. He put it in the Mason jar and turned the lid, with a rubber sealer between metal and glass. The doctor looked, fascinated, at The Avenger's hands. They were not large, and the fingers were slim and white. But they had tightened on that lid till only a machine—or the same slim, white fingers—could ever unscrew it again.

"The Laddex Co. is on Eighth Avenue," mused Benson. "This apartment is on Eighteenth Street between Eighth and Ninth. This man walked home, so—"

"How do you know he walked?" demanded the detective.

"It is rather improbable that anything of so bizarre a nature could occur to him in a subway," Benson quietly pointed out. "It is possible, but not probable: crowded subways are not the best spots for murder."

"Then it *is* murder?"

"Of course. Again figuring probabilities against possibilities. It is possible that something like this, entirely new to medicine and science, could suddenly appear full-fledged and kill. But it is not probable. Almost certainly, some human agency produced this for purposes as yet unknown. Therefore, the man's death will be classed as murder; since a man-made thing killed him."

"Braun walked home," Benson resumed. "His path was almost certainly along Eighth Avenue. I would check back the length between here and the Laddex Co., if I were you. See if anything in the least unusual is in evidence over that distance. Also list every building and its tenants, along the route. Particularly the west side of the street: the Laddex Co. is on that side, and Braun's place is west of Eighth; so it is probable that he walked down that side."

"Yes, sir," said the detective, instinctively using the tone usually called from him only by the commissioner, himself.

He went out. The last thing he heard was Benson saying: "Doctor, if I were you, I'd use that disinfectant of yours *again.*"

And in The Avenger's tone was more emotion than you would have thought could exist behind that cold, immobile face and the icy, impassive eyes.

The homicide man, like a diligent operative, checked the Laddex Co., as well as Eighth Avenue between the firm and Braun's street.

He found nothing at the company, as Benson's tone had already indicated. The foreman repeated his statement that Braun had been perfectly well when he left. So did the man's fellow workers and the night manager.

The homicide man retraced his steps down Eighth Avenue. On his way up he had listed the firms along it. He looked once more for evidence of anything peculiar on the sidewalk, itself, as he went back down.

He did not see the glass fragments beside the Sangaman-Veshnir Building, and he couldn't be blamed for that. The capsule had literally smashed to dust when it hit. The tiny fragments were thinly scattered. Braun had seen them because he'd been looking for something specific in one restricted area.

Completely puzzled, and with shivers chasing themselves up and down his spine as he thought of the snow man, he went to headquarters to report.

As he went, he unconsciously scratched at the back of his hand.

CHAPTER V

The Powdered Menace

The drugstore was on Sixth Avenue and Waverly Place. From the outside it looked all right, except that the store part seemed a little small for the space the total business appeared to occupy. But inside, it was very unusual indeed.

The store part took up less than a third of the total floor space. All the rest was occupied by a large rear room.

Along one wall of the room was a workbench on which was as much paraphernalia as could have been seen in the big laboratory of the Sangaman-Veshnir Drug Corp., itself. Beakers and retorts and Bunsen burners were side by side, with glass tubing and jars of mysterious compounds.

Along the other wall was a similar bench. But the first long table had chemical apparatus laid out on it, while this second one was cluttered with all the things an electrical engineer might need for the most advanced experiments.

At the back of the room, taking up about equal spaces, were finished results from the two long tables. There was a cabinet full of vials containing drugs and chemicals such as no ordinary chemist dreamed existed. Beside this was another cabinet which did not open but which had a screen for a front. This was a television set more perfect than any commercial laboratory would be able to put out for years to come.

At the chemist's side of the strange room was working the proprietor of the freak drugstore, Fergus MacMurdie.

Mac was about six feet tall but looked taller because he was so angular and bony. Knees and elbows were knobbed and protruding. Protruding, too, were his ears, which were like sails. His skin was reddish and coarse, with big, dim freckles just under the surface. His eyes, though, took away any humor of appearance.

MacMurdie's bleak, hard blue eyes, set like stones in his homely Scotch face, reflected the tragedy of his life; loss of his family when a racket bomb exploded in one of his drugstores. Since then, he had worked for The Avenger against crime, having been set up in this drugstore by the immensely wealthy Benson.

Mac had the glass Mason jar, brought by Benson from Braun's apartment, on the workbench. Beside it were ranged a super-mircroscope, weighing half a ton, various gelatins used for bacterial culture, and an ordinary piece of beefsteak covered, it seemed, with fine snow crystals: the same stuff that had made a snow man out of Braun.

He turned.

"*Whoosh,* mon!" he exclaimed. " 'Tis altogether the most dreadful stuff I've ever seen under a lens."

The man he addressed, lounging in a chair in front of the big cabinet that had a screen over the front, was named Algernon Heathcote Smith. But if you wanted to stay in one piece, you never called him that. You called him Smitty.

Smitty was a Hercules. He stood just three inches short of seven feet tall, and weighed two hundred and eighty-five pounds. He had a fifty-three-inch chest and reduced haberdashers to despair by calling for size nineteen collars. He looked as dumb and good-natured as he was big; but the looks didn't mean anything.

The underworld could have testified as to how good-natured he was! As to looking dumb—Smitty was an outstanding electrical engineer. It was for his genius, indeed, that the bench across from MacMurdie's had been outfitted; and it was his genius that had devised the marvelous television set at the rear of the room.

"It fairrr gives me the shiverrrs," the Scotchman burred, scowling at the snowy stuff.

"Looks like ordinary confectioner's sugar to me," said the giant, Smitty. "Or dandruff," he added.

"Heaven grant ye never have dandruff," Mac said.

"Got a report on it yet?" said Smitty, glancing at a high window in one wall of the lab. The things that went on in here were not for public view; therefore the windows were set more than head high. It was dawn outside.

Mac nodded his sandy-reddish head.

"Yes, I have a report. Will ye get the chief for me?"

Smitty switched on the television set. He waited a moment for it to warm up. Then he said, at the screen:

"Smitty and Mac reporting, chief."

There was a minute in which nothing happened. Then the screen seemed to fog over. The fog gathered into form and became a face.

The face of The Avenger.

White as linen, dead as wax, terrible as a poised sword, the paralyzed face stared from the screen. In it, steady and emotionless, the eyes burned forth.

"Yes, Smitty, Mac."

"I've analyzed the stuff ye sent me, chief," Mac said. "Leastwise, I've got a sort of preliminary report as to its nature."

"Well?"

"It's impossible, chief. If I hadn't seen it, I'd not have believed it. The stuff's a kind of mold. It grows like lightning. The spores are dust-fine; they hang in the air for minutes before settling to the ground. They seem to be a kind of bridge between the animal and the mineral kingdoms."

"Artificially cultivated, Mac?"

"Yes! I'm sure of it."

"Go on!"

"It doesn't act like other molds. It doesn't fasten on jellies or decayed substances. It attacks only one thing. That is, meat. And only fresh meat, too. When disintegration has set in, it refuses to germinate on it. Oh, 'tis a very snooty kind of stuff, this mold."

"Any more?"

"On meat, it reproduces fastest, like I said. It has hair-fine feelers. No—finer than any hair. Ye have to use the big microscope to see them. The feelers go down into any tiny irregularities—"

"On a human body, then," Benson cut in, "I suppose the pores and hair follicles would be attacked?"

"That's right, Muster Benson. If the stuff got on a person's body, it would kill him in a hurry. It would clog all the pores, which is enough for death. But more, it would of course sift into the lungs and coat them, too. So ye'd have a phenomenon like pneumonia, only faster than any pneumonia could ever worrrk."

"One more thing, Mac. I have my own opinion on this point, but I want yours, too. Is the stuff deadly to the public at large, do you think?"

"Muster Benson," said Mac urgently, "it's the deadliest thing I've ever had the bad fortune to look at! I'm sure it's contagious. I'd say that any mon gettin' some of it on him —even a bit as small as a pinhead, would die. He'd die fast or slow, dependin' how little of it stuck. 'Twould take a longer time to cover him. But—die he would!"

"Then?"

Mac said the thing that had burned in his bitter blue eyes since first examining the snowlike substance:

"If any of this mold gets out, Muster Benson, we may have an epidemic that would make the Black Plague, in the Middle Ages, look silly. Because, d'ye see, some people escaped from that. And from this—no escape. One touch is death!"

Mac chewed his lip, then asked the question he scarcely dared put into words.

"Has . . . has anybody been exposed to this?"

"Yes, Mac, several have," Benson said quietly. "And I'm afraid we'll be hearing from them soon."

Into headquarters marched the doctor who had been called by John Braun just before he sank into the coma of death. The doctor's face and lips were the color of ashes, but he was calm. It was, however, the calm of a brave man past all hope.

He went to the commissioner's office.

The commissioner normally wouldn't have been up for three hours yet, for it was half past four in the morning. But he had come down in a hurry at the report of the "snow man." There are some things you can *feel* are terrible, even if they seem meaningless and fantastic at first. This was one of them. It called the commissioner to his duty.

"You attended Braun?" he repeated, to the ashen-faced physician. "I see. I meant to get in touch with you first thing in the morning. You have something to say to us?"

"I have," said the doctor. His voice was like his face—perfectly composed, drained of all emotion. Even of terror. "Rather, I have something to show you."

He took overcoat and suitcoat off. He unbuttoned his shirt and let it hang from his belt. Under that was a white undershirt, of the athletic type. But the commissioner, half rising from his chair in horror, didn't look at the athletic shirt. He stared at the doctor's arm.

The arm, from wrist to shoulder, seemed to have been turned to snow.

"Good heavens!" whispered the commissioner. "You, too—"

"I touched Braun, of course, in the pursuance of my examination," the doctor said steadily. "I washed in the usual strong disinfectants. It seems they weren't strong enough. I have what Braun died of."

"You've seen other doctors? There is something you can do?"

"There is nothing on earth I can do," said the doctor quietly. "Except to die! I think that will happen in about six hours. Evidently just a little of the white substance got on my hand. It took a long time to spread to the elbow—but a much shorter time to go to the shoulder. Now, if you look carefully, you can see it spread even as you watch."

"There *must* be something, man—"

"I have kept my arm literally bathed in strong germicides. It hardly even slows the stuff! I have kept scraping it off. It comes back immediately! Indeed, it does little good to scrape it because that doesn't get the growth from the pores; and it is this that is deadliest."

"But, man alive, if this gets around to others—"

"That's why I came here, instead of waiting for death at my home. To warn you. You must sequester everybody who went near that corpse—keep them quarantined as people have never been quarantined before. You must get hold of every one even thought to have contacted them. You—"

The commissioner's phone rang. In the urgency of the physician's visit, the commissioner was disposed not to bother to answer. But finally he did.

The homicide man whom the doctor had called to the Braun apartment was on the wire.

The detective was a brave man, too. He had shot it out with gunmen, risked bullets and knife-blades. But he wasn't as brave, in the presence of a microscopic organism that looked like snow crystals, as the physician was.

He was screaming, was almost incoherent. He had gibbered into the phone for over a minute before the two got what he was driving at; though their intuition whispered the message to them before the detective's words did.

The detective had suddenly remembered, a few minutes before, that *he* had touched the corpse, too. He had just barely brushed it with the back of his hand. So he had gotten up from bed and turned on the light.

His hand and wrist and part of his forearm looked as if unseen hands had gently sifted powdered sugar over them.

CHAPTER VI

Crossed Trails

Sangaman, broken fugitive from the law, stared out the window of his retreat.

Veshnir's Maine cabin, so kindly put to his use, was an elaborate place. Log cabin it might be; but it was two stories tall, contained eight rooms and two baths, and had its own electric plant including water pump.

It was in about the center of the thousand or so acres of almost virgin Maine woods that went with it. No soul was in that area, save for Sangaman himself. You couldn't see a hundred yards clear in any direction because of the thick trees. About a mile to the east was the seacoast; but along here the coast was as deserted as the woods.

It was the perfect hideout for—a murderer.

Sangaman, staring absently out the window, had aged ten years in the hours succeeding the murder of Targill. He had been a rich man, respected, prominent in business and society. Now he was a hunted thing, with only a little in cash that he had managed to withdraw secretly before he fled.

His brain had cleared a bit, and he was pretty sure, now, that he had *not* murdered Targill. Still, he could not *swear* that he had not done it.

But if he had not—then who had? There were two theories to follow that. One was that some employee had sneaked into the laboratory, unknown to the others, and killed Targill. The other was that Veshnir had done it!

The first must be discounted because Veshnir had vehemently maintained that he had seen Sangaman attack Targill.

The latter appealed most to logic.

But there was no sense in Veshnir's killing Targill. There was, it seemed, no motive. Also, if Veshnir had done it, and framed it on him, why wouldn't he turn Sangaman over to the police instead of hiding him up here in this wilderness? That didn't make sense, either.

Guiltless or guilty, Veshnir had hidden him. And hidden he would remain till something, somehow, broke on the Targill case. In police custody, he was doomed. Free, he still had a chance.

Back in New York, in a fine Park Avenue apartment, a girl was reading about Sangaman. The girl was tall and slender and had chestnut hair. Her face, though youthful and feminine, was slightly like Sangaman's sensitive face. And that was natural enough, for she was Sangaman's daughter, Claudette.

She read with horror: Targill, head chemist at the Sangaman-Veshnir Drug Corp., murdered. Thomas Sangaman missing. His partner Veshnir, loyally denying that Sangaman was in the building that night, although the building employees stated otherwise. Sangaman's fingerprints found on the murder weapon.

A little moan came from Claudette's lips. This was her father they were talking about! Her father—a killer! It was impossible! She must prove otherwise. But how? The police were no aid. They had already judged her father guilty. Who, then, could she go to?

Claudette Sangaman was one of the rare few in private life who knew of The Avenger, and she knew that he specialized in giving just that kind of help: aid that the regular police could not or would not give.

Twenty-five minutes later she stood before the center door of The Avenger's huge headquarters on Bleek Street. Over the door was a small sign in black and faded gilt. The sign had but one word on it:

JUSTICE

She went in, and up to the top floor after being passed by a small, lovely blond girl with sympathetic eyes. Claudette Sangaman gasped, as most people did, when they saw The Avenger.

The white, dead face was like a mask under her gaze. The icily flaming, colorless eyes bored into hers like diamond drills as she stumbled forth on her plea for help. Help to clear her father.

She was precisely the kind of person The Avenger lived to help. But this time she had come to him at a very unfortunate moment. The Avenger was deeply sympathetic, but his flashing brain was occupied to the exclusion of everything else by the case of John Braun.

The case of the snow man.

That, he feared, would take every ounce of his energy for an indefinite number of days—

There, Benson stopped short. His eyes took on the pale glitter that touched their depths when his genius found a small, significant point to fasten on.

Thomas Sangaman. Sangaman-Veshnir Drug Corp. And a chemist had been murdered.

"Nellie," Benson called in his quiet but vibrant voice.

Nellie Gray came to him. She was the small and lovely blonde who had first met Claudette.

Small and pretty, she was just a shade over five feet tall and slim for her height. She had bronze-gold hair and gray eyes, and a complexion that made her look like a pink-and-white doll.

Dainty and tiny and soft appealing looking—but Nellie

Gray was an expert in jiujitsu and wrestling, and could even box pretty well. She could fight like a little tigress, and had belied her fragile appearance more than once in her work for The Avenger. Furthermore, she was almost as uncanny a marksman with rifle and automatic as The Avenger, himself. She had picked that up from her archeologist-explorer father—murdered by criminals of the type Nellie helped Benson work against, now.

"Nellie," said Benson, eyes stabbing in her direction with their pale glitter, "please bring me the list of firms on Eighth Avenue made up by the detective who died this morning."

Nellie brought the list. The Avenger glanced at it and read aloud:

"Sangaman-Veshnir Co., lower Eighth Avenue."

"That's right," said Claudette, hope lifting at this renewed interest after his refusal. "That's the address of dad's company."

"That's on the west side of the street."

"Yes," said Claudette.

"About four blocks from the Laddex Co.," Benson mused, "and fourteen or fifteen block from Braun's street."

Claudette didn't know what he was talking about, now; so she said nothing.

"Is the laboratory, in the Sangaman-Veshnir Building, on the Eighth Avenue side?" Benson asked.

Claudette nodded. "On the top floor," she added.

The Avenger's machinelike brain clicked the pieces into correlation with each other, and formed a plausible whole.

John Braun had died of a mysterious thing that The Avenger was sure was man-created. The kind of thing that must have come from some laboratory. It was logical to suppose that John Braun had passed under the high window of such a laboratory on his way home—to death! And in that laboratory a highly expert chemist had been murdered, for some reason or other, that same night.

It looked as if the trails crossed. One was the path up which you might toil to rescue Sangaman, if innocent. The other the trail to the origination of that dreadful white stuff that turned its victims into snow figures.

Here, the paths intersected and became one.

"I'll help you!" said Benson.

CHAPTER VII

Pig In Pants

The Sangaman-Veshnir laboratory and top-floor offices had hummed with police and reporters all day. The man who had been murdered in there was not so important; but the man who had done the murdering was. Thomas Sangaman! That was a big name; so the police were appropriately busy.

At eleven o'clock the night after the murder, however, the activities had simmered down. Examinations and visits by news correspondents were completed. The place was officially sealed and was empty. So was the building, save for the night watchman and an assistant engineer—just as it had been the night before, when the head chemist was killed.

At a little after eleven o'clock there was movement on the roof of the building adjoining the Sangaman-Veshnir place. That building was seventeen stories high, just two lower than the Sangaman-Veshnir Building.

Two men crept through the night from the fire escape to the opposite edge of the roof. One loomed noiselessly along like a great ship sliding through a black harbor; that was Smitty. The other trod like a soundless gray fox; that was The Avenger.

At the edge of the roof, The Avenger drew a length of fine cable, made of specially treated silk, from under his coat, fixed a small, tool-steel grappling hook to it, and threw the hook up twenty feet so that it caught over the cornice of the Sangaman-Veshnir Building.

The two men drew themselves up hand over hand, then unhooked the special little grapple. At the front edge of the nineteen-story roof, Benson fastened the grapple again, and without turning a white hair at the thought of the two-hundred-foot drop to the sidewalk below, he lowered himself to one of the Sangaman-Veshnir laboratory windows.

The window opened under his slight tug. You don't lock windows nineteen floors up. Next moment both men were in the laboratory where Targill had been murdered.

The mode of entrance was typical of The Avenger. He had a magic name. He could have entered any place, police-sealed or not, by the mere mention of wanting to. But if he entered a place with police permission, he had quickly learned, the fact he was working on that case instantly got out to the papers. Every police reporter has a friend at headquarters.

So The Avenger worked habitually without police knowledge.

Inside the laboratory, behind the sealed door, Benson snapped on a powerful little flashlight.

The laboratory didn't look as it had when Targill died the night before. Then, there had been several flat trays, carefully glass-covered, with the stuff in them that looked like snow. Now, there were no such trays. Last night there had been a small rack of the snow in glass capsules near the bench at the front window. Now, there was no such rack.

There was, as The Avenger swiftly found out, nothing whatever to indicate that the stuff which turned corpses into snow men came from this laboratory. He had hardly expected to find open traces of the white stuff. Yet there should be some key to it.

There was a huge refrigerator in one corner. He went

to it. Half a hundred little vials and jars were in there—stuff that had to be kept cold to be preserved. And there was also a large piece of fresh liver.

The colorless, awe-inspiring eyes examined the bit of meat intently. The presence of the liver might mean a mere experiment with the pancreas in an effort to perfect a diabetes cure.

Or it might have something to do with the meat-attacking white stuff.

One thing The Avenger always searched thoroughly when he went through a suspected place was wastebaskets. People, even cautious ones, are prone to throw the most damaging scraps into them either absent-mindedly or because they may be pressed for time.

The equivalent of a wastebasket in a laboratory is the white, metal-covered waste can. So Benson went to that. He opened the lid.

The can was empty.

Near it was an enameled door in the inside wall of the lab. On this were the large, raised letters: Incinerator. The laboratory, being very modern, had a special chute direct to the basement, and the fire. It looked like the end of that trail. But The Avenger was methodical.

Just on the chance, he opened the chute door and played his flashlight down.

"Smitty," his quiet, vibrant voice sounded in the dimness.

The giant came to him, wondering why an empty incinerator chute could be interesting. But the chute was not empty.

Following the beam of the light down a few feet, Smitty saw what seemed to be a lump of fine white snow as big as a small child. Something had been thrown into the chute that was a bit too large for it, and had stuck in the first bend.

"Those tongs, over there," Benson said, nodding his virile white shock of hair toward a tool rack.

The giant stepped to it, came back with the tongs. They were like fire tongs, only not quite so big.

Very carefully Benson drew out the thing that had stuck in the chute and deposited it on the floor. And Smitty checked a sudden exclamation of surprise.

The thing was a small pig, covered with the terrible whitish mold he had seen in the Mason jar on MacMurdie's workbench. But there was more than that to make the little animal remarkable.

It wore pants.

Over porcine middle, and covering the small hams, was a garment made roughly of bath-toweling that was unmistakably a pair of trousers.

"Why in the world," breathed the giant, "would anybody put a pig in pants?"

"To be methodical," answered The Avenger. "Terribly, murderously thorough and methodical."

"But—"

With the tongs, careful not to touch the whitish stuff with his hands, The Avenger took the pants off the pig.

"Yes," he said, "that's the answer. The pants were put on before the animal was exposed to the mold."

He pointed with the tongs. Where the toweling had been taken from the dead pig, the white stuff was tightly molded to the constriction of the fabric.

"The experimenters in this laboratory," Benson said, face as emotionless as ice, "presumably Targill and Sangaman, wanted to find out whether the mold spores would penetrate normal clothing. They put the garment on the pig to experiment. And the spores *do* sift through fabric. They are dust-fine, as Mac reported. You see what that means? Whether a person is naked or clothed, all his body will be reached by the fine spores if any of this stuff is around. Clothes are no protection at all."

Smitty whistled softly.

"In that case," he began, "a pinch of it in a crowd of—"

He never finished the sentence. Suddenly the light flicked out in The Avenger's hand, and his steely, slim fingers compresed on the giant's forearm.

There was a sound at the door!

Both faced that way. The sound was unmistakable: some one was fooling with the lock.

"The window—" Smitty breathed into Benson's ear.

But The Avenger's hand tightened in a negative gesture on Smitty's arm. If the police had been entering, Benson would have slid out to avoid being discovered. But the furtiveness with which the lock was being manipulated convinced him that someone besides the police was at the sealed laboratory door.

Some one stealing secretly in here to get something. If that person could be caught—

Instead of heading for the window and the slim cable still trailing up to the grappling hook on the cornice, he headed for the door. There the two took up their stand, with the giant on one side and The Avenger on the other. Whoever came in here was going to have a surprise.

It developed, however, that the surprise was, for once, going to be the other way around!

The door finally opened, a hand slid along the wall past Smitty's shoulder till it found a switch, and light flared in the laboratory.

Smitty grabbed the hand, and then yelled: "Watch out, chief!"

The most capable of men are sometimes caught off-base by an unpredictable event. It was so in this case. Benson had prepared to capture the one or two or three men who were sneaking into the laboratory for some furtive reason. What neither he nor anyone else could have foreseen was that, not just a couple of men, but a young army of them, was coming into the room!

Smitty held in his vise-like grip the one who had turned on the lights. Benson held another man as helpless as a child. But more came on!

Men boiled in through the doorway till the lab seemed to be half full of them. At least twenty. And all converged on Smitty and The Avenger.

They were all about the same type—stocky, heavy-shouldered fellows with fleshy, foreign-looking faces and close-cropped hair.

The Avenger threw the man he held at the approaching squad and stooped in a lightning-swift movement. His hands jerked from holsters at the calves of his legs two of the world's most curious weapons.

One, from the right leg below the knee, was a little .22 revolver that looked like a slim length of pipe with a small bend for the butt. It had a silencer on it. Benson, with bleak fondness, called the deadly little gun Mike.

The other, from a sheath strapped to his left calf, was a specially designed throwing-knife with a needle point and a razor edge. The handle was a hollow tube, which gave it an arrow flight when it left The Avenger's grim hand. And this weapon, he called Ike.

One of the foreign-looking men had an automatic out. Ike flashed forward like a silver bullet from The Avenger's left hand. The blade deftly sliced the man's knuckles so that he dropped the gun with a yell.

Mike, the special little .22, spat out a small slug. The shot could hardly be heard, but the man next to the one who was nursing a dripping hand went down as if he had been slugged. Which, in effect, he had been. The .22 bullet with marvelous accuracy, "creased" him—hit the exact top of his skull so that he was knocked out instead of killed. The Avenger, even in moments of stress, followed his iron-clad resolution not to take life himself.

But the two out of the running were only two drops in a very large and active bucket. There were nearly a score left. And they were on the two before Mike could do more than spit out one more leaden pea and send a third man to the sidelines.

There was no more appearance of guns. Evidently the one Benson had silenced had been a hotheaded error. These fellows didn't want any sound of gunshots to bring people around. Silently but furiously they swarmed at Smitty and The Avenger.

The giant knocked down two, with two blows that came so fast they seemed like one motion. He got a third by the neck, lifted him off his feet, and hurled him at a fourth. The Avenger, meanwhile was clubbing with Mike.

The little gun, even as a club, was deadlier than you'd imagine. It was a slim steel length, with silencer and all, of about ten inches. In swift, scientific taps, it cracked down; and with every venomous, deft crack, a man sagged to the floor.

But two men, even such as these, couldn't overcome twenty. A concerted rush by the attackers, who were skilled fighters themselves, took the giant off his feet. And Benson swayed and went to his knees, too. A blackjack glanced off Smitty's skull, bringing a gasp to his lips.

Benson's hand dipped into his pocket and came out with something like a small handful of glass marbles. He dropped one on the floor at his knees, and threw the rest with a scattering motion.

There was a succession of tinkling sounds as they broke. And the light in the laboratory began to fade out.

The men fighting the two broke their silence, then. One of them cried out in the surprise of seeing an electric cluster of lights slowly dimming, for no discernible reason. A couple of the others swore in a guttural foreign language.

The lights kept on dimming.

With a movement that was really no more than a blur in quickly gathering gloom, The Avenger retrieved Ike, the throwing-knife that had pierced the wrist of the first gunman.

No words needed to be exchanged between Benson and Smitty. The two always worked in perfect unison. Smitty knew all about what had happened: The Avenger had broken half a dozen of the "darkness" pellets he always carried with him. The pellets released a black pall so impenetrable that even electric lights were quickly blotted out by them.

These were blotted out now, less than thirty seconds after the release of the ink-black liquid within; liquid which had such an affinity for oxygen that it volatilized instantly and spread as an odorless, tasteless black gas.

The air was as black as the water is around a squid after it has discharged its concealed ink. In the blackness, Smitty and Benson got to the window. Benson went up the silk cable to the roof; while Smitty, helped by darkness, held the groping enemy at bay. Then Smitty kicked over the workbench under the window with such force that it knocked his attackers down like ninepins, and joined his chief on the roof.

They drew up the silk cable. But they did not go. One of The Avenger's most often-used tactics was to apparently flee—but actually stay near and return to the scene. He did so now.

They heard the laboratory door slam. The men who had so unexpectedly overwhelmed them were getting away, fast, carrying their wounded with them. Then Benson silently slid down to the laboratory again.

A little of the black pall was settling. It did not last long. It was light enough for him to see what he wanted to. And that was a thing he'd been pretty sure he'd see.

The mold-covered pig was gone!

The men had come in here to look around and make sure that no incriminating trace had been left in the laboratory by the person who had killed Targill last night. They might not have found the pig in the incinerator chute. But they had gotten it, now, through Benson's having lifted it out to the lab floor.

It was logical that further examination of the laboratory would not reveal the secret of the frosted death. Benson swung out of the window and back up the cable to join Smitty on the roof.

CHAPTER VIII

Silent Partner—Silenced

The residential section called Clapham, out on Long Island, is for the very rich. The estates are larger, the grounds of each better kept, and the servants more profuse, than in any other spot.

One of the biggest of these estates belonged to a man named August Taylor.

August Taylor, sixty-seven, a semi-invalid and a most irritable and unpleasant man, was remarkable for three things. One was that he possessed nearly twelve million dollars. Another was that no woman had managed to grab him as a husband; so he was a bachelor with his money-bags. The third was that he had four million dollars sunk in the Sangaman-Veshnir Drug Corp., which in a way made him a silent partner; and he also had himself insured for another three million with the corporation as beneficiary.

August Taylor did not often show up at the Sangaman-Veshnir Building. He let his millions represent him there. For the most part, he rarely stirred from his Clapham estate. And that was natural enough. The estate was a beautiful place in which to spend all one's time.

At the moment, however, on the morning after the night

raid on the Sangaman-Veshnir laboratory, old August Taylor was not enjoying the beauties of his surroundings.

August Taylor was dead!

Four doctors, distinguished specialists whose names were known wherever medicine was practiced, were gathered around the body.

Taylor had died of something that no one of the four of them knew anything about. It was something that made his body look like it had been covered with powdered sugar. They were busy examining the strange phenomenon now, fascinated as specialists always are by something new in diseases, and at the same time feeling a little afraid.

A gray-haired doctor with rimless spectacles scraped some of the white stuff from the dead millionaire's cheek. In a moment the cheek was covered again, with no clear space showing.

"It's a kind of mold," he marveled. "But mold is usually bluish gray—this is white. And what is mold doing on human flesh?"

There was a silence; then a man named Caldwell said: "The mold evidently gets into the lungs, too. That accounts for the symptoms resembling those of pneumonia."

They all looked pretty grim. The whitish mold, that looked like fine snow, or powdered mica, was pretty dreadful stuff. And they recalled reading about an odd fungus death in New York. As physicians, they had more than an inkling, now, of how terribly they had misjudged when they touched the whitish stuff.

As if on signal, they all turned and raced for the luxurious bathroom. They washed in carbolic solution, so strong that burns resulted. Caldwell suddenly looked at his right hand. It seemed that the middle knuckle of his second finger was whiter than it should be. But that might have resulted from the powerful disinfectant he had just used.

Fergus MacMurdie could have told them that carbolic did no good. He had experimented with every known germicide in an effort to get hold of something that would be an antidote for the frosted death. And as yet he had found nothing.

Any disinfectant strong enough to kill the fungus was more than strong enough to kill living flesh, too; to eat it away, burn it up, shrivel it.

The mold was a low-grade organism practically indestructible. You could freeze it at two hundred degrees below, Fahrenheit, and it didn't hurt the spores. In this respect, it was not too unusual: there are several low-grade organisms able to stand even the absolute zero, and the airlessness, of outer space. But in addition, this whitish stuff could take treatment that would destroy any other known form of life.

Yet there must be an antidote for it. There must be something to combat it! MacMurdie dared not let himself think otherwise. There *had* to be— with the white death loose in the great city. If not—chaos!

So Mac, with eyes black-rimmed from lack of sleep, was working night and day in his drugstore laboratory to find the answer.

Meanwhile, The Avenger was tackling the thing from the human angle.

At the moment, he was in the anteroom of Veshnir's big top-floor office. He had passed the door of the laboratory in which he had been so busy the night before, with his eyes impassive and inscrutable. He had given his name to Veshnir's secretary, in the anteroom.

Veshnir came out himself, staring at the white, dead face and the colorless eyes of his visitor with his own face benevolent, sad and kindly-looking.

"I've heard a little about you," he said. "And I've heard that you were interesting yourself in the tragedy we have had around here. I'm very glad to see you at such a time. Come in."

He stood aside for Benson to go into his private office, then followed him in and closed the door.

"I can hardly realize all the things that have happened,"

Veshnir went on, as he waved Benson to a chair, and seated himself behind his desk. "Terrible. Terrible!"

"Yes, they are," said Benson, icily colorless eyes fastening on the man's kindly face like diamond drills. "Especially the frosted death!"

"Frosted death?" repeated Veshnir. Then he nodded. "Oh, yes. The thing the papers have been hinting at. But—what is it, precisely, Mr. Benson?"

In a few words, Benson told him what it was. Veshnir's face paled.

"But why do you connect that dreadful thing with this place? Surely you don't mean—"

"It is almost certain that it originated here. In your laboratories."

"Good heavens! But what makes you think that? What proof have you?"

The Avenger told him that, too, eyes like drills on Veshnir's benevolent face.

"It simply doesn't seem believable," Veshnir breathed, after a moment of silence.

"You know nothing of such experiments, then?" Benson said quietly. "I had hoped you could shed some light on the white mold."

Veshnir spread his hands. "I never even heard of it before. But that's not so odd. I am in the sales and personal-contact end of the company. I have little to do with the laboratory—sometimes don't go into the place for months at a time, even though it is right next door. So I wouldn't necessarily know of their experiments. Sangaman—"

He stopped abruptly and looked confused.

"Your partner?" said Benson. "What about him?"

Veshnir slowly took a cigar out of a box, lit it, and exhaled a thin puff of smoke.

"I was about to say that Sangaman was in and out of the laboratory all the time. He did quite a bit of work in there himself, personally. He came up from the ranks—was a fine pharmacist. But I can't believe he had anything to do with the horror you describe."

"Could the murdered man, Targill, have perfected such a thing without its being known by you or Sangaman?"

"All things are possible, of course," Veshnir said oracularly. "But I doubt it."

"It is conceivable, wouldn't you say, that Sangaman suddenly found out the terrible nature of Targill's latest experiment, and killed him to prevent its ever leaving the laboratory—but killed him too late?"

Veshnir swung his chair till he was looking out the window. He stared out at the sky, smoking thoughtfully. Then he stared into the icy, dangerous eyes again.

"I have never believed that my partner murdered Targill," he said firmly. "I don't believe it now. But if he did it—and I say *if*—it would only have been for some such compelling motive as that."

"Sangaman's reputation in business circles is good," Benson said evenly. "How is it with you—his partner?"

"I don't like to say anything about that," Veshnir replied, with a look of distress on his kindly face.

"I would much appreciate an answer."

Few people could defy that tone in The Avenger's voice. Veshnir didn't try to.

"Well," he said reluctantly, "Sangaman has always been inclined to practice . . . er . . . sharp dealing. I've covered for him several times. Nothing illegal, you understand. Just things that are slightly unethical. I've been going over the books since all this stuff has come out, and I've found quite a few traces of such dealings. There was one item about 'crude drugs' to a foreign power that can only have meant the shipment of war goods to that nation. I hadn't known about that before."

He shook his head a little.

"But when it comes to murder—and to a guilty knowledge of an experiment as destructive and awful as this frosted-death thing—I simply can't believe it of him!"

Veshnir, it seemed, was outside the whole affair. There appeared to be nothing to get from him. The Avenger thanked him, in his even, quiet voice, and left.

Late papers were on the street as he came out of the building. The three-o'clock edition, with streaming headlines, announced:

MURDER ON LONG ISLAND
FROSTED DEATH APPEARS AGAIN

Benson got a paper and skimmed the account with about three glances of his photographic eyes.

The newspapers, it seemed, did not share Veshnir's firm refusal to believe in Sangaman's guilt.

The police, in searching through the home of the dead man, August Taylor, had found one thing that did not belong there. That was a pair of rubber gloves. They had turned the gloves carefully inside out and found prints of the extreme tips of the fingers last in them.

The prints were those of Thomas Sangaman!

So there the authorities had it cold. Sure evidence on a human being who was beginning to show up as a fiend from hell.

He had been only a murderer with the first crime: for he had killed Targill more or less normally. But when he murdered Taylor, the accounts ran on, he revealed himself as a demon. Because he killed deliberately with the frosted death as a weapon!

These things were now clear:

Thomas Sangaman *had* killed Targill. There could no longer be doubt about that.

Sangaman had killed him, almost certainly, to get hold of the result of an experiment—the deadly whitish stuff.

With that as a lethal weapon, Sangaman had sneaked into Taylor's home. Handling the stuff with rubber gloves, he had put some of it on the old man, and then fled.

Why?

The motive was crystal-clear, too.

August Taylor was a silent partner in the firm of Sangaman-Veshnir. That corporation, it had recently been revealed, was on the verge of bankruptcy. A partnership insurance policy of Taylor's would now save the firm. That was why Sangaman had committed the second murder. It proved him to be either mad or stupid, as well as criminal. For if the murder could be proved against him, of course, the policy would never be paid out.

More significant than the news content, was the *tone* of the account. Never had Benson read in a newspaper such bitter, cold fury. Sangaman was a monster! He had helped invent a thing that might turn into an epidemic such as had never been seen in modern times. He had murdered to get sole possession of the secret of it. Then, with it, he had committed a second murder.

Sangaman was a cold-blooded beast. He didn't even deserve the formality of a court trial. If he were ever caught, he should be taken out and lynched.

Looking at that account, The Avenger knew that everybody reading it would be infuriated to the point of insanity. If Sangaman ever were found, he would be torn to pieces by the first people who saw and recognized him.

Benson rolled the newspaper and tapped it reflectively as he went toward Bleek Street. In the lurid columns he had read one very significant thing. It gave meaning and clarity to the whole bizarre performance. It told him almost everything he needed to know.

CHAPTER IX

The Clouds Of Death

Claudette Sangaman was at Bleek Street when Benson got there. She was in one of the big leather chairs in that enormous top-floor room. She was crying hysterically, and Nellie Gray was trying to give her the comfort that only another woman can give to a woman in despair.

When Benson came in, Claudette made a heroic effort and calmed herself a little. But the calm was perhaps worse than the hysterics. White-lipped, she pointed to a copy of the latest paper at her feet. It was this, evidently, that had brought her here.

"Have you read that, Mr. Benson?"

The Avenger nodded, colorless eyes like ice in his white, dead face.

"The lies! The dreadful lies! Why, that paper makes my father out as *more* than a murderer. If he is ever found now, he will be shot on sight! Oh, what are we going to do?"

Benson's face, white, terrifying, still, could never express emotion. Only his eyes could show that. The glints in their colorless depths became more pronounced now, in sympathy, as he stared at the stricken girl.

"Has anything been accomplished, yet?" she pleaded. "Anything at all?"

The Avenger nodded, dead face like a wax mask.

"Much has been accomplished," he said.

Nellie Gray stared quickly at him. She hadn't known anything important had turned up, yet. For of course she knew nothing of the message Benson had picked out of the recent, bitter newspaper account.

"What?" asked Claudette.

"Mainly, I am morally certain now that your father is innocent of Targill's murder."

The words seemed to make ripples in the ensuing silence of the big room, like a heavy stone dropped in a mill pond.

Claudette almost collapsed again.

"You're sure of that, Mr. Benson?"

"Dead sure!" said The Avenger.

"Why then everything's all right, and we can go to the police—"

"Not yet," Benson said regretfully. "I know he is innocent. I expect to prove it. But as yet—there is no scrap of evidence to take to headquarters."

The girl slumped back in her chair. But her chin was up now, and her shoulders no longer drooped. The Avenger had that effect on people. Because he was such a driving, sure force himself, he made others feel sure.

"I am counting on you," she said, getting up after a moment. "I *must* count on you! I have no one else in all the world to turn to."

"You have no family save for your father?"

"That's all," she said, unsteadily. "Just dad. When . . . if . . . he dies, I'll be all alone."

"Keep your courage up," Benson said. "I'll hope to have something soon to tell you."

She went out. And the Avenger's icily flaring eyes followed her till the door was shut. Their almost colorless depths were strangely clouded for a moment. Something was trying to fight its way into his mind. Something that disturbed him very much.

It had to do with the meaning he had picked from the newspaper story of Sangaman's guilt in the Taylor death. He knew that much. And something else. Something the girl had just said—

Benson could move almost faster than the eye could follow. Occasionally there are such men—with a co-ordination of mind and whipcord muscle that makes the motions of others seem slow. The Avenger was like that.

He got to the door almost before Nellie Gray was aware that he had left his chair.

"She mustn't be allowed to go down this street alone!" he snapped, eyes like flashes of stainless steel. "Of course! I should have known it at once! She is in terrible danger."

"You want me to—" Nellie began.

"Stay here!" he rapped out. "There may be phone calls—"

He was gone, racing down the stairs with more urgency than Nellie had ever seen him move.

He got to the street door, over which was the small Justice sign, just as Smitty was coming in. In fact they almost bumped.

"Smitty! With me!"

The giant turned and ran after Benson down the short block composing all there was to Bleek Street. He couldn't quite keep up with the gray fox of a man with the dead face, but he did his best.

They got to the corner, where traffic was thick. Ahead, Benson saw the girl, walking toward a cab stand.

Probably there wasn't another man in all the great city who could have seen the thing. But those colorless, keen eyes of The Avenger's had telescopic power. He saw it, inconspicuous as it was.

Claudette was just raising her hand to call a cab from the line when it happened.

From some window near her, something flashed out and down. The Avenger couldn't see what it was. It was too small. But he knew. The crystalline flash of it told him. He couldn't see what window it came from, because he was looking down along the street at a thin angle. But he let that problem go till later.

The flashing downward arc of the little thing made Benson spurt forward with even greater speed. He was probably covering ground at a rate of nine seconds flat per hundred yards, when he got to the girl.

His steely arm swept around her before she knew he had approached. She cried out in surprise. As she did so, the little glass capsule whose flash Benson had seen, hit the sidewalk next to both of them.

There wasn't anything dramatic about it. The thing hit with a soft, harmless-sounding little *plop* and broke into a million pieces. That was all.

But that small *plop* was more terrible to discerning ears than any roar of a bomb explosion would have been.

Benson leaped away with the girl as if she had weighed only a few ounces. He didn't stop till there was twenty yards between him and the bit of sidewalk where the capsule had broken.

"Why—" gasped Claudette. "What do—"

The Avenger didn't pay any attention to her. He had a more urgent thing to do, now.

People were beginning to gather, as people always do when something a little out of the ordinary happens. And this had been out of the ordinary: a man with blazing, colorless eyes and snow-white hair, catching up a girl and running twenty yards with her as if he had suddenly gone crazy.

Some of the people were pressing ignorantly toward the spot where the capsule had hit. They didn't see what Benson saw. And even Benson might not have seen it had he not had an inkling of what to look for.

From the spot on the sidewalk where glass lay in fragments, a kind of gray cloud was rising. It was like a genie rising from a bottle, to solidify later into hideous form. Only this wouldn't solidify. This would stay that way, faintly shining, a whitish mist, looking innocent and harmless—till flesh and blood were near.

Then—

"Back everybody!" The Avenger's voice was like the crack of a bullwhip. There was such command in it that everyone in earshot stopped in his tracks as if a hand had been laid on his shoulders.

Then they moved again. People are like that, too. You can't make them obey a command for any length of time without telling them why. And Benson couldn't take the precious seconds to try a real explanation.

"Poison gas—around that doorway!" he called in his whiplash voice.

That did it. The crowd shrank hastily back from the doorway near which the dreadful, white mist was hovering in air. A few with extra-good eyes saw the mist, and talked volubly about the spectacle to the rest.

"Smitty!" The Avenger rapped out.

The giant turned from the light gray cloud.

"Nearest butcher shop," Benson snapped. "Get a side of beef—any big chunk of meat. Bring it here instantly!"

There was a butcher shop on the far corner. The giant raced for it, running as fleetly as a stripling, for all his great size.

"The . . . frosted death?" whispered Claudette, staring with fearful eyes at the faint, shimmering mist.

"Yes," said Benson. "Aimed at you! Fortunately it is still, without wind, at this moment. So the stuff stays where it is. If a breeze were to spring up and scatter it before Smitty gets back—"

The giant was on his way back, already, with a quarter of beef, running as lightly with it as if it had been a pork chop. He reached the corner and looked at his chief. Few words were needed between The Avenger and his aids!

Benson nodded toward the gray cloud. Smitty tossed the beef so that it hit at the base of the patch of faintly shining mist.

The result was as weird as it was horrible.

The shining, translucent patch suspended in the still air began to funnel down on the meat like water streaming through a faucet. It was as if the microscopic particles composing the misty patch were little particles of steel, and the beef was a powerful magnet.

In less than half a minute there was no trace of the thin grayish cloud. It was all on the meat.

The crowd couldn't understand that at all. Poison gas, this man with the emotionless, dead face and icily flaring eyes, had yelled. And some had seen the "gas" cloud. But gas settling like that on meat? It seemed *worse* than gas. Now that the danger was over, had they but known it, they all got back to an even safer distance than when it had hung by a thread over their unknowing heads.

Benson drew a deep breath, as the crisis passed.

A uniformed patrolman was hurrying toward the crowd. He started to pass Benson, saw the white, still face of The Avenger and his awesome, colorless eyes, and stopped.

"You, Mr. Benson!" he said respectfully. "What's wrong, sir? It must be important if you're here."

"It is," nodded The Avenger. He put his lips close to the patrolman's ear, so that the words wouldn't be overheard by others and start a panic.

"The frosted death!"

The cop's hands clenched convulsively. He knew more than most about the frosted death. He had been a close friend of the homicide detective who had been unfortunate enough to let the back of his hand brush against the body of John Braun.

"There?" he whispered back. "That stuff?" He pointed to the beef, which was beginning to look as if invisible hands were slowly sifting powdered sugar on it.

"That's right. Listen, and follow instructions to the letter. Get more men and rope this area off. Then get kerosene—gallons of it—and pour it over that side of meat. Burn it where it is. Don't try to take it to the city incinerator or anyplace else. Burn it on the spot!"

The patrolman's face was the color of putty.

"Oh, no!" he said. "Not me! I wouldn't go that close to it for—"

"It's all right as long as you don't actually touch it," said Benson. "We've found that out about it. When it has once settled on something, it fastens there. It doesn't float off, even for another vicitm, by itself. Unless a bit of it is actually placed on your hand, you'll be all right. Just keep from actually touching it."

"I'll say I will," exclaimed the cop, sweat glistening on his forehead.

He blew his whistle for help in keeping the crowd back, and The Avenger and Smitty and Claudette Sangaman moved off. The girl was brave. She was pale, but composed.

Benson saw a cab driver he knew he could trust. He waved him over and held the cab door open.

"Go home," he said to Claudette, "and pack a few things, then come back to my place at Bleek Street. I don't want you to show your face outdoors for the next few days."

"You think there will be more attempts?" faltered the girl.

"I know there will be." The Avenger turned to the driver, a stalwart young fellow with a twisted nose who looked like a thug but with whom you could have left a thousand in cash, uncounted, and have known you'd get it all back again.

"Mike, go into Miss Sangaman's apartment with her while she packs. If anyone—servant or friend or anyone else—tries to get near her, knock him into the next room."

"Yes, Mr. Benson," said the driver.

The cab rolled off.

Smitty and Benson soon found the window from which the glass capsule had been tossed. But it told them nothing. The window opened onto a long-vacant office in an old building next to an apartment house. Prints in the dust had been smudged. There were no fingerprints or clues of any kind.

Benson called the Sangaman-Veshnir Corp., and got the personnel manager on the phone. He asked if any executive, or anyone connected with the laboratory, was absent at that moment.

There was, it seemed. A chemist named Mickelson, now elevated to Targill's place with the latter's death and formerly Targill's assistant, hadn't come in that afternoon from his lunch period. All the rest were there.

"Complications?" said Smitty, as The Avenger slowly hung up the receiver.

"I don't know," said Benson, eyes icily thoughtful. "A new piece in the puzzle, at least. But we'll make it fit, before we finish."

CHAPTER X

Hope—And Defeat

The curse of the frosted death was spreading, slowly but inexorably.

It spread slowly because every health and law department in the city was concentrating on checking it and quarantining those even suspected of having been in contact with it.

It spread inexorably because such a deadly thing *couldn't* be quite corked up.

Here a woman, servant to August Taylor who had touched her master when he called in the early morning for help, died with helpless doctors in attendance. There a man, boarding at the home of the detective who'd touched Braun, and who had been with his friend in death, saw hands and arms turn to snow limbs. In another home, over a big delicatessen store with a foreign-sounding name on it, half a dozen men suffered and died of the frosted death without daring to call doctors at all.

These latter were those of the crowd that had jumped Smitty and Benson in the laboratory. They hadn't been told the full nature of their task and had ignorantly touched the dead pig.

An epidemic slowly, ominously getting started that would

be worse than the Black Plague of the Middle Ages if it were not stopped. It was like a black storm cloud—no, a white, smothering one—that was slowly spreading a pall over the city and obscuring the clear and healthy sun.

While all this was going on, a man sat at the soda fountain in MacMurdie's drugstore, and methodically and endlessly consumed maplenut sundaes.

The man was a tall, gangling Negro, and so sleepy-looking that he was instantly nicknamed Sleepy.

"Ah'll take 'nuther one," Sleepy said. The boy behind the fountain looked at him in awe. He had had four maplenut sundaes already. And his long, skinny, Negroid body was so thin you'd have thought they would show.

"They's sho' good," the colored man added.

He didn't have to talk like that. Joshua Elijah Newton was an honor graduate from a famous college. He could talk as excellent English as any professor, and he did when among friends. But when with strangers or in public places, Josh talked and acted as people expect Negroes to talk and act. It was good protective coloration.

"It's only when a houn' dawg barks that folks pay attention to him," he often said. "When he sleeps in the sun, they let him alone." For Josh was a dusky philosopher with a deep store of wisdom.

Furthermore, Joshua Elijah Newton, no matter what he looked like, was one of The Avenger's aids—and an invaluable one. Josh and his pretty wife, Rosabel, had helped in many a desperate fight with criminals too brilliant for the regular police to handle.

It was Josh's habit, when waiting for orders, to hang around in Mac's drugstore. And while he was there, he saw no reason for not indulging in his consuming passion—maplenut sundaes. He downed them till, as Mac sometimes said: "Mon, 'tis a wonder ye don't look like a string of beads with all those sundaes in ye, one on top of the other."

Mac appeared at the door of the rear room now.

"Josh," he called softly.

There were no customers in the store. If there had been, Mac would not have openly called and Josh would not have openly entered the laboratory. As it was, Sleepy eyed the last third of the maplenut sundae sadly, and left it to go to Mac. Mac shut the big lab door behind them. The dour Scot was red-eyed from continuous work.

"I've got it!" he said.

Josh instantly shed his sleepy look. His eyes shone with clear intelligence—and with an admiration too great to be put into words.

"You have? You're sure?"

"I'm sure!" said Mac.

"If that is true, you should have statues put up in your honor all over New York! You're a great man, Mac."

"There'll be no statues, because no one'll ever know," Mac said wearily. "As for bein' great—I'd call it just stubborn, that's all."

Josh looked at a dozen cuts of meat on Mac's lab workbench. Each was covered with the powdered sugar that spelled death—except the last one. That one was fresh and clear, without the white mold.

"You've found the exact nature of the stuff?" he said.

"Yes," nodded Mac.

A fine brain had been snuffed out when that first doctor, the one who attended John Braun, died. He had guessed immediately the type of thing that had smothered Braun. He had deduced the species of fungus, if not the exact type.

"It's a new thing, Josh," Mac said. "But very, very close to a well-known one. Selectively cultivated from it, I should say. In all but appearance and action, the mold is identical with saccharomyces cerevisiae, or brewer's yeast ferment."

"So the most harmless things," observed Josh, "can be turned into the deadliest weapons—if the minds of men desire it."

"Yes! Here's an instance of it."

Josh stared at the one piece of meat not covered by

the mold.

"And you've actually found the antidote for it? Something to stop it?"

Mac nodded, too tired for superfluous words.

"Then we must start phoning at once—give the formula to every doctor and laboratory in town—"

"That's the catch," said Mac. "There's no formula to give. This antidote isn't a chemical to be mixed up, Josh. It's a living organism, itself. A kind of parasite that attacks the white mold and devours it. Having devoured it, the parasite withers and dies. It can be cultivated swiftly—as swiftly as the mold. But only from its own kind."

He pointed to two small jars, full of blue-green stuff.

"That's the stuff that will do the trick. Applied to a victim of the frosted death, it will eat out the mold in half an hour. There's enough in those two jars to give a bit to every laboratory in the state. From that bit, each can cultivate his own supply."

"Two jars?" said Josh, eyes narrowing.

"Yes. You know why. One for each of us to carry to Bleek Street, to the chief, for distribution. Are the men still near the store?"

Josh nodded.

He had been sitting sleepily at the soda fountain devouring maplenut sundaes, not alone to be on hand if needed—but, also, to watch from the window.

He had been in the store for three hours. And all of that time there had been several foreign-looking men idly propping up building walls, nearby.

Somebody knew, somehow, that experiments with the white stuff were being conducted in the back of the store. And somebody had sent a guard to surround the place.

"A jar for each of us to carry," Mac repeated to the tall, gangling Negro. *"One of us must get through!* No matter how many try to stop us."

Josh nodded, eyes clear and alert. Then they clouded.

"You have worked a lot with this deadly stuff," he said. "Are you sure you're all right? Uncontaminated?"

"I'm all right," Mac said. "The stuff's funny. The spores will get to any meat within ten yards. But the developed mold won't leave that meat, even for other meat, unless actually carried off by touch. And ye can be sure I've not touched the frosted death! I've even worn medicated felt pads up my nostrils so I won't take a chance on inhaling any. No, I'm all right. And so will the city be—if one of us gets through with the antidote."

"This is something well worth dying for," Josh said.

"We can't afford to die! We've got to get through, I tell ye!"

"I'll go out the front way—"

"That's the most dangerous," Mac argued. "I'll take that way."

"It's least dangerous," said Josh, who could be as twisty as a Philadelphia lawyer when he wanted to gain a point. And he wanted badly to gain this—to take the most risk. Mac was more valuable than he was, he thought. "In broad daylight, on a crowded street—who would try anything?"

Mac wasn't quite taken in, but there was no time for arguments.

"All right," he said. "You go out the front way, and I'll take the rear. But—*get through!*"

Josh picked up his small jar as if it had contained gems. But even that was a poor simile. The contents of that jar were many times more priceless than a pint of diamonds.

He went out the laboratory door into the store. With the moment of his exit, he became sleepy-looking again. He shuffled, looking as if he were too lazy to lift his huge feet clear of the floor. He ambled to the street door as if he had nothing on his rather empty mind but his black, kinky hair. He stepped out onto the sidewalk—

Josh Newton could fight like a black panther, and was as fearless and fast as one. But he was undone by his natural conviction that no group of men would try anything fantastic at the store entrance, right on crowded Sixth Avenue, in clear daylight. They'd follow him, of course, he reasoned, and try for him in a less conspicuous spot. And that was all right. If they followed him, Mac would have a better chance.

He hadn't realized the caliber and fanaticism of the men they were up against. And so he didn't have a chance at all!

The moment he stepped from the store, a man who had been standing flat against the wall clubbed him down with a gun barrel. Josh hadn't even had time to see him out of the corners of his eyes.

There were dozens of people within a few yards. Most of them saw the act. Most of them yelled or screamed. The man didn't seem to mind it a bit. As if he were alone on a desert island, he calmly gathered Josh up and carried him toward a sedan that swirled with machinelike precision to the curb.

Three other men, who had been the loungers noticed by Josh at the fountain, came at once to the car. They didn't pay any attention to the crowd, either, till two men more daring than most in such emergencies, tried to hold them while yelling at a cop down the block. Then the men with the phlegmatic, foreign-featured faces coolly clubbed them down, then went on to the car.

The door slammed with a thump, and the sedan drove off. The patrolman, taking in the situation at a glance, knelt and sent shot after shot at the car. It didn't even hasten its pace. It was as bulletproofed as a tank. It went around the corner and was gone—with Josh and one of the two jars that meant salvation for a great city.

Mac, mercifully, didn't know of the swift tragedy in the front of the store. He was going through a tunnel from the rear.

The tunnel, a corridor in the basement of the building behind the store, opened onto Waverly Place, around the corner from Sixth Avenue. It was customarily used by The Avenger when he came to see Mac; so few knew of it.

The men loitering near its street door didn't actually know of it. They were just part of a corps that was acting with all the military precision of an army in battle.

Yes, there were men near the door of the corridor. But there were also men clear around on Fifth Avenue, and more men were stationed on the street north of Waverly Place.

The entire block had been surrounded, coldly, methodically, to guard against just such an exit as Mac was trying to make from some unknown, secret areaway.

However, because the men nearest the exit didn't know of its precise meaning, Mac got a little farther than Josh had. He stepped from the tunnel and got twenty feet toward a cab when the men saw him. Then, without a sound, they rushed him.

Mac had seen a lot of criminal activities. But he had never seen anything like this. For it exceeded the merely criminal. It entered the realm of war, of the military. These men weren't just a gang, they were parts of a machine, with no thought for themselves at all if only their objective could be gained.

Two of the three reached him at the same time. Mac knocked one down with his bony fist that was like a mallet swung at the end of his long arm. He tripped the second—and staggered back to his knees under the impact of the third.

He was up again as if on springs. He managed to elude clutching, clawing hands, and raced toward the other side of the street, and down toward Fifth Avenue. He changed his course in the middle of the street and doubled back again.

One of the square-shouldered men with close-cropped hair was waiting for him on the opposite sidewalk. As Mac turned, the man whipped out a gun, and braced it on his left forearm, evidently deciding that bullets would be the best remedy in the situation.

At this moment a plain-clothes man, who had seen the lawless attack with mouth open in incredulity at its utter boldness, hit the man in a flying tackle. The gunman went down with his gun flying from him.

Mac didn't even see that. He was too busy trying to thread a way past two more men between him and Fifth Avenue, while behind him the original three closed in.

" 'Tis an arrrmy," he groaned to himself.

In the distance, clear at the corner of Fifth, a cop appeared and began running to help. A man down there stepped out, and with no expression on his face, clubbed the cop down.

Mac began to feel utter hopelessness. In the face of this kind of organization, he began to feel that a dozen cops, wading in shooting, couldn't save him. And he was pretty close to right!

However, he couldn't be downed, now. Not with the precious jar of antidote in his possession. He hit the two men ahead of him, running at full speed. One whirled to the curb and sprawled at full length. The other was knocked out of the way.

Still another man stepped from a building entrance; one Mac never did see. With the grim coolness of a military machine instead of a human being, he clubbed the Scotchman. Mac fell! Before he had hit, two of the robotlike men had him by ankles and shoulders and were carrying him toward a sedan. A car that sagged on its tires like an army tank.

The second jar of antidote was gone!

CHAPTER XI

From The Depths

Far up in the Maine woods, miles from even the smallest villages, there was a cleared glade that, from the air, appeared to be just what it was: a landing field.

The landing field was about a quarter of a mile from the Maine coast. It was in the heart of over a thousand acres of almost impenetrable timberland which was privately owned and hence seldom trespassed upon.

On each corner of this field, tonight, there was a landing light that was strong, but so shielded, that it merely glowed without sending rays up into the sky. Like four huge glow-worms, they bounded the space.

A plane coasted for this space. Motors were cut off so that, with its minimum landing speed, it made hardly more noise than a gigantic moth. It hadn't made any noise for quite a while previously, either. The pilot had started down from twenty thousand feet, and from that altitude you can coast silently for many miles with your motors cut.

At the controls was a man who was tall and lean, but otherwise bore the same stamp as the foreign-looking fellows with the phlegmatic countenances. His face wasn't exactly cruel. It was simply hard, humorless, unhuman. He wouldn't inflict pain just to get pleasure from it; he would inflict it because it seemed necessary, and because it simply didn't occur to him to get excited about the pain others might feel.

In the passenger seat was Carl Veshnir.

The man at the controls spoke, and his tone brought out another fact about him. Whoever he was, he was very highly placed in some sort of occupation other than business. For he treated Veshnir, who was rich and usually kowtowed to, as if he were some sort of inferior errand boy.

"I hope, for the comfort of all concerned, that this will be soon successfully concluded."

His English was precise, but his accent was guttural.

"We ought to be done in a week," Veshnir said.

The man's eyes took on a fanatic look.

"Let us hope you are correct. For if you are, you will be rich beyond your dreams. As for us"—his harsh voice took on a biting edge—"we shall change the course of history in a month!"

Veshnir stared at him, eyes genuinely puzzled.

"I can't understand you fellows," he said. "And I can't understand what you hope to gain. Say you capture all the area you wish. The people originally owning it are still there. You can't execute twenty, thirty, fifty million people. All you can do is hold them in slavery. But you can only hold them while your power is at its peak. The minute a flaw appears—and every system shows a weak spot somewhere, in time—your slaves rise and overthrow you. Then the map is as it was before, and eventually all the blood and steel you've spent is forgotten as if it had never been."

The man's eyes flamed in a way that made Veshnir a little sorry he had spoken his thoughts aloud.

"What we capture we shall keep—forever." He stared ominously at Veshnir. "It makes some difference to you, perhaps, what we choose to do?"

"Oh, no," said Veshnir hastily. "Not at all. You fellows have fought each other for two thousand years. I suppose you'll do it for another couple of thousand. But it's no concern of *mine!* It's a long way from *me.*"

"I shall fly you back in say—three hours?"

"Right!" said Veshnir. "And there won't be many more trips needed."

He left the plane and the hidden landing field and struck off through the woods. There was a very faint path to follow, but he followed it easily. This was his path and his woods.

He emerged at the luxurious log cabin, bought and held in a phony name, and knocked on the door.

It opened, and a gun poked against his stomach.

"Oh! It's you," said Sangaman, putting the gun down.

He shut the door after Veshnir and followed him to a rustic divan. He sank down in it as if utterly exhausted. His hands were still trembling from the emotion roused by that knock on the door.

"I can't take this life much longer," he said. "I'm going back, give myself up. Better to be in jail facing a murder charge than here—"

"*Two* murder charges," said Veshnir quietly.

"Two?" Sangaman fairly screamed it.

"And responsibility for many more deaths than that," Veshnir nodded, his kindly face an incarnation of sympathy.

"I don't understand—"

Veshnir told him, hand laid gently on the older man's shoulder. Told him about the spread of the frosted death. Told him of August Taylor's murder, and of the rubber gloves that implicated him. Told him of the public conviction that since he had murdered Taylor by means of the frosted death, he was therefore responsible for the deadly loosing and spread of the stuff.

"Why, this is incredible!" moaned Sangaman. "And hopeless. I thought I was in deep before. I'm in ten times as deep now, with all these things laid at my door!"

He stared swiftly at Veshnir.

"The death of Taylor releases a lot of badly needed insurance as capital for the corporation," he said.

Veshnir shook his head.

"No, it doesn't. Because everyone thinks you did it, and a beneficiary can't profit from his own murder. Taylor must have been killed by somebody for a personal reason. And it puts a different face on the whole thing."

The suspicion died in Sangaman's lined face. He looked hopefully at the partner he had always distrusted because of his chiseling tendencies, but now regarded as his only aid.

"I saw you strike Targill down," said Veshnir. "But this second murder, which you couldn't possibly have done, suggests a very unusual, but possible thing. Suppose some employee of ours were on that top floor that night, with no one the wiser. Suppose he wanted Targill out of the way, and he managed to remove him by drugging you into a partial coma in which you killed Targill? Then, we will say, he wanted Taylor out of the way, too. So he killed him and again implicated you by leaving your rubber gloves in Taylor's home."

"But what motive would any employee have for killing Targill? Or Taylor?"

Veshnir shook his head.

"That's something I can't even guess at, for the moment. But it gives us something to work on—and something to hope for. I'm going to follow up that possibility with every private detective I can get my hands on. Meanwhile, it will be wisest for you to keep on hiding here. Now, more than before, it would be fatal for you to show yourself. And I mean fatal! I doubt if you'd ever get to a jail alive, if you were captured. Public opinion is rather strong against you at the moment."

Sangaman had looked eighty years old when Veshnir came in. He looked ninety when Veshnir left.

Veshnir, on the contrary, walking back down the woods path, looked more contented—and benevolent—than he had when he came.

Everything was going perfectly, thanks to his quick, shrewd brain. In a week or less the whole thing would be over. At that time, Sangaman could be—eliminated, too. It could be done in such a way as to make him the goat in the final, most outrageous act of all.

Then Veshnir would go his way, enormously richer, above suspicion, with Sangaman shouldering the entire responsibility in his grave.

He veered from the path to the landing field, and went down an even fainter one to the left. He wasn't going back to the plane for a little while yet. He had another goal in mind.

Not far from the landing field, on the coast, there was a small inlet that made a natural bay. On the shore was a remnant of a dock, where a fisherman had kept his boat till discovering that tides and storms made the bay unusable during too much of the year.

In this little bay, a black hulk rose furtively to the surface. First a periscope, then a conning tower, then a wedge-shaped black hull. Men swarmed out of the hatchway onto the deck of the submarine, and a small boat was swung up and set into the water. The captain of the undersea craft stepped into the boat without a word and was sculled ashore.

CHAPTER XII

The Automatons

The shack was about forty feet square. It was sided with tarpaper, and in the gloom of the forest, was impossible to see for more than a hundred yards. On top of the squat, one-story structure, were tree branches in a perfect camouflage from eyes that might peer down from a plane.

A corner of the building was walled off into a kind of crude office about eight feet square. In this, Veshnir met the submarine captain.

The captain gave Veshnir, without a word, a blue-green slip of paper of the type checks are printed on. But it was twice as large as our ordinary checks. It was a foreign draft on a New York bank, made out to Carl Veshnir, for "crude drugs."

"This," said the sub captain, voice hard and humorless and efficient, "is a token payment, only, to guarantee our good faith. The real payment, shortly to follow, will be placed in our name in your bank, and later switched to your account secretly and over a period of months so that its size will rouse no comment. That was your wish, I believe?"

Like the plane pilot, he treated Veshnir as an inferior. But Veshnir didn't notice that. His hand was greedy as he clutched the draft. His fingers closed like a miser's clasp on a stack of gold coins. Only this represented many, many golden stacks.

It was a check for one million dollars!

"The radio," said the captain, "has brought code messages of trouble in your New York. Trouble, I gather, directly resulting from your—work. There has of course been much excitement. Some have been sacrificed, and more will be. I trust you won't let sentimentality interfere with our plans?"

"What do you mean?" said Veshnir, looking at the check.

"I mean that the most natural thought would be for one to disclose the whole secret of the . . . er . . . trouble to police headquarters, in an effort to prevent more deaths. Yet that cannot be, my friend. Publicity, at this point, would ruin our great, historical program beyond repair."

"There will be no publicity," said Veshnir.

"You swear that? You promise that . . . er . . . sympathy for those unfortunate enough to have come in contact with our weapon won't move you to tell what you know in an effort to stem the spread?"

"I'm sorry for the people," said Veshnir. And in some queer way he managed to express real regret in his tone. "But—talk to the police? Try to help? With nineteen more million dollars to be mine in a few days if I keep still? Hardly! It isn't necessary to swear, with nineteen million to glue my lips shut!"

"It is good," grunted the sub captain, with a veiled look in his fanatical eyes. "After we have concluded our vast program, it will be all right to help the authorities. By then some thousands may have felt the white death. But after that it will be all right. And your part will never be guessed."

He bowed like a hinge, in the middle, and walked to the door of the eight-by-eight cubicle.

"May I look around before I go back to my ship?"

"Of course," said Veshnir.

He showed the captain what the tarpaper building contained. And it was like a look into the deepest inferno.

The tarpaper shack was a temporary factory. In it were about ten workmen, and in it a product was being efficiently, rapidly manufactured and stored twenty-four hours a day. But the characteristics of the workmen, and the nature of the product, differentiated this from all other factories, whatsoever.

There were twelve long benches, in rows in the low shed. At ten of them stood a man each. But they didn't look like humans. Their appearance made you believe, suddenly, in zombies—or living dead.

Their eyes were dull and seemed almost incapable of sight. Their faces were vacant and pallid, and indicated that the brains behind them were certainly incapable of thought. Their hands moved like the tentacles of automatons; and like automatons they never slackened their movements. Minute after minute they made the same moves, without slackening pace, and almost, it seemed, without looking.

The moves made by them were bizarre in the extreme.

Before each was a long, shallow tray which was half filled with chopped meat. Over the meat was growing, with incredible rapidity, the white mold. Beside each pan was a smaller tray. In these trays were piled little glass capsules about as large as the tip of a man's thumb.

The robotlike workers were filling these capsules with the mold.

With a small instrument much like a tiny teaspoon, white mold was skimmed from a bit of the chopped meat, and packed in a glass container. Then the little glass capsule was sealed with a drop of collodion. After that it was set aside, to be taken to a rack that covered one whole wall. In that rack was tray after tray of the capsules. Unguessable thousands of them, with the swift-growing white stuff reproducing itself endlessly and fantastically in the meat trays —to be made into still more death pellets incased by glass.

A curious thing was to be noted. The glass capsules freshly packed looked as if they were filled with snow. The capsules that had been packed for several hours or more, seemed, instead of fine snow, to have silver-gray dust in them.

That was because the mold, deprived of food and forced into suspended animation in the capsules, shriveled into dormant spores just waiting to be released again—in the vicinity of meat—or flesh.

"It is good," said the sub captain, staring with bleak eyes at the thousands of capsules in the rack. "How long has it taken to produce these?"

"Two days," said Veshnir, face never looking more kindly and benevolent than then.

"Five days more should be sufficient," the captain said. "By then we should have twice enough for our needs. It is very, very good—"

He stopped abruptly and stared into a corner he had seen for the first time. One of the twelve long tables had hidden it before.

He glared at two men. One was a freckled, homely Scotchman with bleak blue eyes and ears that stuck out from his sandy head like sails. The other was an extremely gangling Negro who managed to look sleepy and disinterested even in such circumstances.

The circumstances being that both the Scot and the Negro were tied so tightly that flesh at arms and ankles bulged. They were lying like sacks on the rough plank floor.

"Who are dose two men?" snapped the submarine captain, in his agitation forgetting some of the precision of his English.

"Two who tried to interfere," said Veshnir. "Men from your country's offices in New York captured them. We brought them here."

"Why?" demanded the captain.

"Eh?" said Veshnir, puzzled. "Well, it wasn't safe to keep them around New York—"

"Why did you not kill them at once? But no matter. Shoot them now! While I watch. It is very bad to keep living prisoners."

"Oh," said Veshnir. "You mean why didn't we kill them instead of capturing them. Well, it happens I need workers in here. Two of the ones I had died prematurely. As you see, two of my work tables are vacant. So I brought these men to fill them."

"They will never work for you," stated the captain. "You have but to look into their eyes to see that."

"They will," said Veshnir complacently, "when I am through with them. And that reminds me. You have a powerful weapon in the white death. But how are you going to control it? The mold is deadly to all life—not just the inhabitants of some one country."

"We shall cross that bridge when we come to it," said the sub captain. "In my homeland are many scientists. We can develop an antidote to the frosted death before taking over our new slave states in person."

"Your scientists," said Veshnir, "can work on other things. I have an antidote."

"Then," said the captain, "your fortune will be doubly large! We shall pay you for that as well as for the white death when the time comes to use the antidote."

He went on. Veshnir, eyes glittering at all the money he was going to collect in the next few months, came back, after locking the door, and stood over Mac and Josh.

"Ye skurlie," said Mac, through set teeth. "Ye not only let a terrible epidemic spread in ye'r own city, to gain a few measly millions; but ye now have the antidote to it—my antidote—which ye'll hold in the face of spreading death for a few more million!"

It is probable that Veshnir could not have watched a rabbit killed without wincing at the blood. But he could think of many human beings dying, with no wince at all, as long as they died out of his sight. There are many men like that, and probably all have the philosophy Veshnir expressed.

"Look," he said, as if arguing with himself rather than his prisoner, "there'll be war soon. There have always been wars, and there always will be. In the war, millions will be killed. But nobody gets excited about that, do they? Then why get excited if a few hundreds, or maybe thousands, have to die in New York over a war weapon? There are a hundred and thirty million people in this country. Do you really think a few thousand more or less will make any difference?"

"Skurrrlie!" burred Mac, writhing in his bonds.

"Suppose I made cannon," Veshnir went on. "They would kill as many as this new weapon. But I would be respected and looked up to just the same. I don't see that I'm doing anything so wrong."

"A few minutes ago I'd have called ye a gangster," grated Mac. "But ye're worse."

Veshnir shrugged, then turned to the table nearest the men. There was a tray on the table. And rubber gloves, elbow length. Veshnir began working the gloves up over his forearms.

"A little damage will be done," he said, "till the nation buying the mold has captured what territory they please. Then they will spread the antidote over there, and I will see that it is passed around over here. After that, everything will be all right. My customer wins a war, and I live out my life in a vast fortune."

"A fortune built on the foundation of thousands of your own countrymen's bodies!"

"Think what you like," said Veshnir. "You'll help in my plans just the same."

Josh spoke up, holding his eyes open as if by a great effort from the claims of peaceful slumber.

"How's that, boss? We goin' to wuhk fo' you-all?"

"That's right," said Veshnir. He stared curiously at the Negro.

"The report is that you are a trusted aid of this man, Benson," he said perplexedly. "And you were trusted with one of the two jars of the antidote. That seems odd to me. You don't look very bright."

"Oh, I'se smaht 'nuff," said Josh smugly.

Veshnir shrugged.

"It must be that Benson thought you were so inconspicuous that you'd be a good messenger boy. But thanks to the method and efficiency of my foreign friends, it didn't work. If that jar of antidote had gotten to State hands, all our plans would have failed."

"What you-all pay fo' wuhkin' here?" said Josh.

Veshnir smiled coldly.

"That's rather humorous, if you had intelligence enough to realize it," he said. "You won't be in condition to appreciate wages while you're with me."

Mac stared with new eyes at the ten men working in the low building. Their automaton actions. The lack of intelligence in their eyes. Their clay-colored faces and lead-colored lips.

"The white mold," Veshnir said, "is primarily a war weapon. The little glass capsules of it, rained down from planes, will capture a nation in short order. But Targill and I discovered a curious little incidental use for it."

The gloves were in place. Veshnir took up a long, slim glass tube, about the size of a soda-fountain straw. He dipped it into the mold on the meat tray.

"Targill and I," he went on, "discovered, by experimenting with animals, that if a small bit of the mold is lodged at the base of the nasal cavity, the spores work up into the brain. There, they devour the surface cells. In the process, the person's power of conscious thought is taken away from him, as in certain types of brain illnesses. The spores work much more slowly on the nerve cells than on muscle fibers. The person will live four days to a week, after lodgement of the spores in the nasal cavity, where he would die in a few hours if the spores started on the body surfaces."

"But during the four days to a week," Mac said steadily, "the victim is a kind of robot? Like these men in here?"

"That's right," said Veshnir.

"And ye intend to make automatons out of Josh and me? And worrrk us at those two vacant tables?"

"Right again," said Veshnir, looking kindly and benevolent. There was whitish mold in the end of the glass tube now.

He stepped to Mac's side, with the glass tube in his hand directed toward Mac's face.

Mac promptly seemed to explode into writhing limbs and bucking body. The bonds held him powerless, but they didn't keep him from wriggling around like a cat on a hot stove.

"Everybody. Here," called Veshnir, raising his voice as if for the benefit of slightly deaf ears.

The ten dull-eyed human machines in the place left their tables and came to the dour Scot. With ten pairs of hands on him, Mac was held as moveless as a rock.

Veshnir inserted the tube, and blew into Mac's nostrils. Just once. Very lightly.

He turned to Josh with what was left of the stuff that looked like fine snow in the little glass tube.

Josh was still. There was no need for the ten to hold him. Veshnir repeated the process.

"There," he said, pleasant-voiced, straightening and stepping back. "In about four hours you will be ready to obey orders, without a thought of your own to interfere."

He went to one of the dull-eyed men, already back to their worktables and filling little glass capsules with the frosted death.

"When the clock strikes three in the morning," he said, "release those two and put them to work at the two empty tables."

He went out. Mac glared at him with raw murder in his bitter blue eyes.

But Josh seemed strangely still, and resigned.

CHAPTER XIII

Roof-Top Trail

The many windows in the enormous room on the top floor at Benson's Bleek Street headquarters seemed to have Venetian blinds over them. But they were not Venetian blinds.

The slats were not wooden strips and could not be tilted. They were strips of nickel-steel, set at a forty-five degree angle; so no bullet could penetrate the windows. Their ends were embedded in the masonry of the building.

Through the slits, the flaring colorless eyes of The Avenger stared down from a rear window. The view back there was over the low roof of a one-story garage, fronting on the next street.

There were two men on the roof. They were in regular suits; but their coats were cut a little long, and looked almost like military garments. The erect, stolid carriage of the two men looked military, too.

Benson paced with his panther tread to the front of the room and looked out on Bleek Street.

There were two men across from the doorway, over which hung the Justice sign. There were two more at the dead end of the block. There were three at the opposite end of the street.

The Avenger's face, dead as wax, motionless as gray steel, disappeared from behind the slats of the blind. His colorless, marksman's eyes were as brilliant as moonstones with a light behind them.

This was no crew of thugs. This was no criminal gang. It was something on the order of an army corps stationed all around the Bleek Street headquarters. He was up against the method and precision of a military machine, not fighting unorganized killers.

Nellie Gray watched him from the long table in the center of the room.

"How are you going to get out of here, chief?" she said.

"I'm not worrying about getting out," Benson said. "But I want to get out unobserved. And that seems a bit tricky."

He walked to the television radio and tried once more to get Mac at the drugstore. But the call was unanswered by either Mac or Josh.

"They wouldn't have left," said Benson, "unless Mac had discovered what he was hunting for: an antidote to the frosted death. And if he had found that, they wouldn't have rested till they had come here with it."

Nellie nodded, her shrewd brain pacing his own.

"So," she said, "something has happened to them."

"And to the antidote it is reasonable to suppose Mac found," Benson nodded.

He glanced once more at the two big, square-shouldered men on the garage roof.

"Is Miss Sangaman down on the second floor?" he asked.

Nellie Gray nodded. "She's asleep, poor lamb. Worn out."

"What room has she? I wouldn't want to disturb her."

"The blue room, in front."

"That's all right, then," said Benson. "Unless something goes wrong, she won't hear anything."

He went down to the second floor.

The corridor there ended in the rear, it seemed, in solid plaster and brick wall. But Benson went toward the wall as if he intended to walk right through. Which, as a matter of fact, he did.

He pressed a certain spot. The end of the hall, five by seven and a half, moved a little. The entire end wall was a secret door, leading out onto the garage roof. Out there, serrated edges of red brick, that you would never notice when they were properly in place, moved a bit with The Avenger's push.

Having unbarred the secret door, Benson opened a panel in it which consisted of one brick that telescoped down into the false one beneath it, at the touch of a button. He peered out the little opening.

One of the two men out on the roof was staring over the edge into the narrow areaway beside the garage. The other —glared with startled eyes directly into Benson's colorless ones. He had just happened to be looking right at that spot of innocent brick wall when one of the bricks seemed to melt out of it.

Benson's right hand whipped down to the calf of his leg. It whipped up again with Mike, the silenced, special .22, leveled through the aperture.

The Avenger didn't seem to aim at all. Yet the slug that lisped from Mike's silenced muzzle hit its target within a sixteenth of an inch. As, indeed, it would have to, to conform to The Avenger's rule of disabling but never killing with his own hand.

It went through a stiffly worn derby at precisely the spot to slam against the very top of the man's skull, to "crease" it, and stretch the man out on the roof as unconscious as if he had been chloroformed.

The man had started to yell to his comrade when the bullet clipped him. However, his gasp must have warned the other, at the roof edge, for he whirled and saw his prone accomplice.

The result was funny, in a mad, dangerous sort of way. The man didn't know what had happened. Something had knocked his comrade out, but nothing was in evidence. There was no other person on the roof. On one side was thin air, where the garage fronted. On the other was blank wall for ten feet, and then closed windows of the top-floor room.

The man dropped swiftly to his knees, gun whipping out. He looked all around, trying to see in every direction, at once—and saw nothing, anywhere.

The Avenger coldly and calmly ended his dilemma for him by squeezing Mike's trigger again. The second man went down, unconscious.

Benson opened the secret door, walked out onto the roof, and picked up the nearest of the two. The limp figure was beefy, must have weighed around two hundred pounds; but The Avenger carried him without taxing his superb physique in the least.

He took the man into the building, shut the concealed door tightly again, and carried him lightly up the stairs.

In the big room he nodded wordlessly to Nellie. She knew what the nod meant. She went to a corner and got a small but very compact case and brought it to her chief.

A major miracle was about to occur.

The tremendous nervous shock that paralyzed Benson's face had left it in a curiously plastic state. The features couldn't move of themselves. But under prodding fingers, they could be molded into any shape desired—and would stay there. The result was that Benson had really two names to the underworld. He was The Avenger.

And he was the Man of a Thousand Faces.

He could deftly mold his countenance into the exact resemblance of almost any other face; and when proper color eyes and facial tinting were added, he was that other man.

He prepared to become somebody else now.

He propped up the unconscious man he had brought in from the roof. Beside the man's face, he placed a small mirror. By looking into the mirror, Benson could see his own wax-white countenance close beside the other man's florid face.

He opened the case.

It was a make-up kit such as couldn't be duplicated anywhere outside of a large Hollywood studio. There was a tray in which dozens of tissue-thin glass shells reposed. The shells were tiny cups, designed to fit over Benson's colorless eyeballs. On each pair was painted a slightly different colored pupil. Thus, by selection, The Avenger could acquire brown eyes, or blue, or amber, or any other color.

He slipped a pair of shells with gray-brown pupils over his eyeballs, holding the unconscious man's eyelids open for an instant, to check the color again. Then he began to manipulate the modeling-clay texture of the flesh of his face.

The nose flattened, broadened, became slightly bulbous at the tip. The cheeks became shallower, fleshier-looking. With a careful hand, Benson tinted the result to the high, florid color of the man. Then over his shock of snow-white hair, he drew a wig with close-cropped, light brown hair.

He estimated the height of the man.

"Shoes," he said to Nellie, "with two-and-one-quarter-inch lifts."

He was in the unconscious man's suit when Nellie Gray got back. He put on the height-adding, special shoes and the man's derby, with the two little holes in it where Mike's venomous small bullet had gone in and out again.

And The Avenger was that man!

Benson went through the pockets of the garments he wore. He was, he discovered, a man by the name of Molan Brocker. There was a recently stamped passport in his coat pocket, from a powerful European nation, announcing that fact.

Beside the passport, there was a little money. But there was only one bit of paper of any kind. That was the torn-off corner of an envelope. The corner contained a printed return address. The address read: Klammer Importing Co., Fifth Avenue.

Benson went back down to the second floor and out onto the roof. The other man was still lying there, deeply unconscious. It was possible that he had a mild concussion from the bullet's crease; but his life was in no danger.

Benson went to the edge of the roof. There was a heavy rainpipe there; and it was up this that the two men had climbed in the first place. The Avenger went down the pipe and along the areaway to the street on which the garage fronted.

Two men promptly wheeled toward him from across the street, unconsciously marching in exact unison. Two more came toward him from down beyond the garage. It was so precisely and mechanically done that it was like the changing of the guard.

Benson was so good at judging men that he was almost psychic about it. At a glance he picked the one of the four with the most authority in the set of his jaw. This one he approached at once.

"Brocker!" the man said. "Why do you leave your post? Do you not know—"

The Avenger knew a dozen languages, and knew them so well that he had no accent in any. The knowledge was advantageous, now; the man spoke in the tongue of north Europe.

"There has been trouble," Benson replied in the same language. He had had no chance to hear the real Brocker speak; so he could only guess at the proper, guttural intonation. "The man with the white hair—I believe he has gotten away."

"Impossible!" snapped the authoritative-looking man. "All have been in place in front. And if you and Vogg have been properly on duty in the rear—"

Benson had only been waiting to learn the name of the other man.

"Vogg has been hurt."

"Hurt! There was a fight?"

"No! I don't know what happened. I turned, to see that Vogg was down. I ran to the areaway and looked down. There was a sound that I could hardly hear. I leaped back from the edge with these holes in my hat." He pointed at the bullet holes. "Some one had shot me."

"You saw no one?"

"I was not sure. I leaped back with my own gun out. I thought I saw a man running this way. A man, it seemed, with white hair showing under the rim of his hat."

"No one, of any color hair, has come into this street. I am positive. But this is serious!"

"What shall I do now? Return to my post?"

"Of what use?" said the man bitterly. "If you and Vogg were attacked, it must have been that during the distraction our enemy did, indeed, manage to slip away. Is Vogg badly hurt?"

"I don't think so."

"Then leave him to look after himself. You—report to our superiors immediately. I shall get the rest, and we will comb the neighborhood before we accept, as fact, the white-haired man's escape."

He turned away, and Benson, walking with a stiff and military gait on his high-lift shoes, went down the street.

Report to our superiors!

He had intended only to get away from his headquarters. But with a glance at the men on this street, he had had a swift change of plan. It had seemed like an excellent time to find out a bit about this foreign, efficient corps on United States soil.

Klammer Importing Co., Fifth Avenue.

That might or might not be the headquarters for this ruthless crew. He could only chance it.

The Klammer office building was old, part apartments and part offices. The Klammer Co. was on the fourth floor, walk-up. Benson opened the door there.

He could not make his face express agitation—or anything else. So he did it by the swift pace of his entrance and his hurried tone to the young lady at a desk near the door.

"I must report at once! Important!"

"To whom?" asked the girl, in the same European tongue.

"To whom do you suppose, stupid?" Benson snapped. "Be quick—"

An inner door opened. A man with a paunch and a square-looking head stepped out.

"Very well, Brocker. Make your report."

"The man with the white hair," The Avenger said, making his voice urgent and wishing he could do the same with his moveless face, floridly made up in another man's image. "He has gotten away from us."

"Fool!" rasped the paunchy man. "Do you know how serious that is?" He stepped forward. "Where did he go? Did you follow? Have you any idea?"

"We didn't have the chance to follow. He was too swift."

The paunchy man paced up and down, hands twisting behind his back.

"Who can say where he has gone, now! Who can tell what harm he can work! We have just gotten the last of our reports on the meddler, Benson. They are most disquieting. You pack of fools!"

"We admit it, sir," said Benson meekly, timidly. "And now—your orders?"

"Be at ease. Go where you like, you—" he searched for expletives and couldn't seem to find any strong enough. "You and the others shall pay for this when we get back to the homeland. You know how you will pay."

Brocker gave the salute of the land whose language he was talking and started for the door. He didn't appear to do so, but he moved a little more slowly than he might have. Before he had gotten the door open, the paunchy man whirled to the girl.

"The telephone!" he rapped out. "They must be warned up on the coast—"

Benson went out.

"They must be warned up on the coast." It told him a lot.

The ultimate use for the frosted death had become increasingly obvious, in the last twenty-four hours. It was to be a ghastly war weapon, to be shipped abroad. To the country from which had come these heavy-shouldered, phlegmatic-looking men who worked like a military machine rather than a gang.

Very well, but to be used by that country, it would have to be shipped there first. That meant two things.

The terrible white stuff was being cultivated somewhere in large quantities, and packaged somehow for handling.

It could not be shipped openly. Nor would anyone even try to smuggle it, on a large scale, on regular ships. Too much chance of its being discovered.

What craft could bear it most secretly? An undersea boat. Where would it head in to an obscure port?

"*Up* the coast," the paunchy man had said.

Somewhere north of New York a submarine would be stealing in—if it had not anchored already. Almost certainly near there, some kind of hidden plant would be located, turning out the shipment for the sub.

But Benson shelved this valuable thought for the moment. At the time, that day, that Claudette Sangaman had almost been killed, a chemist at the Sangaman-Veshnir Corp. named Mickelson had been absent. He might have been the one to toss the glass capsule at her—though this would have upset considerably, the theories Benson had formulated. Or his absence might be a coincidence meaning nothing—or a lot.

Benson set out to discover what it did mean.

CHAPTER XIV

Death Sentence!

Andrew Mickelson, of the Sangaman-Veshnir laboratory, had had nothing to do with the glass capsule tossed at the feet of Claudette Sangaman. He hadn't even been in New York at that moment. From an early lunch hour on, Mickelson had traveled, all afternoon and evening, on train, bus, hired car and finally afoot, to get where he was, now.

That place was the forest hide-out of Thomas Sangaman. And Mickelson grinned insolently, menacingly, as he sat on the rustic divan in the pine-walled living room.

Sangaman hadn't met Mickelson with a gun. Veshnir, as far as Sangaman knew, was still around. He had only gone out of here a half hour before. He had thought it was Veshnir coming back, when Mickelson knocked.

However, Sangaman didn't think of it, now, as Mickelson's tap at the door that he had heard. It was the knock of doom itself. That much had come out in a short time.

"So!" Mickelson said, grinning at the lined old face of his former employer, and then grinning at the rustic room. "This is the hide-away! And that puts Veshnir in cahoots with you! I had an idea it would be like that. I'd have bet you were up here."

"How did you know of this place?" asked Sangaman wearily. He wasn't particularly curious about the answer. He felt completely beaten down. "I thought Veshnir had kept it a close secret—"

"Sure! So close that nobody knows he owns a place in Maine—but me. I know it because he wanted it kept secret. I let him use me as dummy. I bought the place, giving still another name, and paying cash Veshnir handed me. I never thought it would mean anything to me. Then you disappear, and I put two and two together and find it does mean something to me."

"What?" sighed Sangaman. "The notoriety of being the man who found me? But if that was all you wanted, you'd have come here with police."

"That's right," smirked Mickelson. He was a spindly man with eyes that could bully, even though they were inherently those of a coward. "It's not fame I want."

Sangaman stared with dawning comprehension.

"It's money," Mickelson said. "And believe me, I want plenty."

"I don't quite understand—"

"Oh, yes, you do!" said Mickelson. "You are wanted for murder. And for a lot more. As long as you stay here you're safe. But if the cops ever get you, you'll go to the chair. That is, you'll go to the chair if you live that long. You're apt to be lynched if the public gets hold of you."

"Well, that is all true."

"Sure it's true! So that's where I come in. You give me one hundred thousand dollars, or I turn you in to the police."

Sangaman sat with his head in his hands. His voice was that of a thoroughly beaten man when he said without looking up:

"I was rich last week. I could have given you that much money. But not now. I fled from New York too abruptly to have been able to bring much money. I have only two thousand dollars with me."

"You can get the rest," said Mickelson threateningly. "And believe me, you'd better."

Sangaman only sat with his head in his hands. Mickelson went on:

"I'll take what cash you have as a first payment. Then you get in touch with Veshnir. He wouldn't have hidden you here if he wasn't willing to help you. Get the rest from him. I'll give you twelve hours—"

The door of the luxurious log cabin opened suddenly. Sangaman didn't even move. He knew who it was: Veshnir. He knew because he had heard the slight rasp of a key in the lock before the door opened; and only Veshnir had a key. But even if he hadn't heard the preliminary rasp, even if the door had been pushed open by the police, Sangaman still would not have moved. He had gotten to the point where he didn't care much if he were captured or not.

Mickelson whirled with his lips open as he heard the door. He half rose from the divan as he saw Veshnir, then sank down again. He glanced defiantly at the other partner.

Veshnir stared back in surprise.

"Well, Mickelson!" he said. Then: "You here! But I remember—you bought this place for me, didn't you? So you would know of my ownership. But why are you here now?"

Mickelson was wary, but aggressive. He jerked his head toward Sangaman.

"I'm here because of him."

"He wants blackmail money," Sangaman said. "He guessed I'd be here, came and made sure; then he demanded hush money if I'm not to be turned over to the police."

On Veshnir's kindly face grew a look of shock. He looked like a benevolent deacon who had been kicked in the shins by a man he was only trying to befriend.

"Why, Mickelson! This from you?" he mourned.

"Why not from me?" snapped Mickelson.

"After all Sangaman and I have done for you—"

"What have you done for me, I'd like to know? You gave me a job, sure. At wages about the same as I'd get in anybody else's laboratory. You paid me a little for a couple of dirty jobs I did for you. But damned little. I don't owe you anything. But *you owe me,* now. One hundred thousand, or the police come here and get Sangaman. And things won't be so hot for you, either. You'll be a murder accomplice, hiding a murderer."

"I'd never have believed there could be such ingratitude," sighed Veshnir.

"Oh, stow it," snarled Mickelson. "Do I, or don't I, get the hundred thousand?"

Behind the countenance of Veshnir, "saddened" that any one could be so unkind, a shrewd brain was clicking out a solution—and a slight change of plan.

Mickelson had to be eliminated. An unexpected source of danger, he was as menacing to Veshnir as to Sangaman. Also, it had begun to look as if Sangaman would have to go, too.

He had been holding Sangaman in reserve, in a manner of speaking. He had meant to let the tired, elderly man live another few days—and then take the responsibility for the death factory in the woods. He'd have had Sangaman's body found there, as if the man had been sole owner of the place and responsible for the frosted death. He'd have made it look as if Sangaman had been murdered by some double-crossing crook who'd been buying the white stuff.

It looked now, however, as though it might be risky to keep the old man alive that long. And, actually, it wasn't necessary. Sangaman could be tagged with the whole affair, even if his body weren't discovered in the plant. His mere disappearance would be enough. And if he were carefully buried here in the trackless woods—

"Speak up," said Mickelson, with the arrogance of the little man who is for once on top. "Do you come through, or don't you?"

"We'll pay," sighed Veshnir, shaking his benevolent head reproachfully. "Tomorrow night—"

"Tomorrow morning, as soon as the banks open," Mickelson corrected him. "I'll be at the laboratory. You can bring the money there, in cash."

"How can you get back to New York from here so fast?"

"I'll be going with you," said Mickelson. "You came here by plane, of course. Well, I'll go back with you—by plane. It will save a lot of trouble for me."

Veshnir clicked that over, in that cold and cunning brain that functioned behind the benevolent face. It was quite satisfactory, he decided.

"All right," he said. "You can come with me. I'm about due at the plane now. My pilot will be waiting."

"Just a minute," objected Mickelson. "I'll have your two thousand here and now, Sangaman."

Sangaman started to reply. But Veshnir cut in quickly, with a protective glance at the older man:

"I'll get the money," he said. "Just wait right here."

Sangaman relaxed, without saying anything. It was odd how he had misjudged his partner. Or, rather, judged him too harshly. Veshnir *had* pulled some shady deals. But no man could be more loyal in a pinch than Veshnir was being. Even now, he was going to save Sangaman's slender store of cash for him. Probably had money out in his plane. Going to give up two thousand of his own rather than see Sangaman, fugitive from justice, stripped of all resources.

But Veshnir did not go to the plane. He went quickly to the sinister, tarpaper building, and came quickly back to the cabin. Just before entering, he took two thousand dollars from a bulging wallet.

Veshnir had had buckskin gloves on before going back into the weird little factory. He still had them on. But now there was a slight difference. Under them, not showing, were rubber gloves.

Veshnir had held the right little finger of his gloved hand apart from the rest, so it would not scrape. He carefully rubbed the sheaf of bills over a part of this finger. Just a part.

Then he went in.

"Here is your money," he said reproachfully to Mickelson. "Though you seem to have forgotten that money ill-gained will bring you to a bad end."

"I'll take a chance on that," smirked Mickelson, counting the sheaf, and putting it in his inside pocket.

Veshnir turned to Sangaman in a stanch-and-true friendly way. He held out his right hand.

Sangaman took it in a thankful grasp.

"Keep your chin up," Veshnir said. "Soon your troubles will be over. Come along, Mickelson."

At the plane, the lean, scarred-faced man at the controls flashed a coldly surprised, deadly look at Mickelson when he clambered into the cabin after Veshnir.

"I did not know we were to have a passenger," he said irritatedly.

"Neither did I," Veshnir said. "But a friend of mine unexpectedly turned up."

The foreign-looking pilot moved his hand ever so little toward his gun. Veshnir shook his head. He gave the man a long, reassuring look. The unexpected friend, that look said, doesn't need bullets. He has been well taken care of.

Mickelson didn't catch the side glance. He had his hand in his pocket, feeling those crisp bills. He was thinking of all the other bills his shrewdness would bring him in the morning.

In New York, with early morning breakfast, he went to his apartment from the plane. He didn't watch behind him very carefully; so he did not notice that here and there men with square, erect shoulders and phlegmatically unmoved faces, gathered and followed him.

When his apartment door closed, the men, at least ten of them, took up stations all around the one building entrance. They stood there like guards.

Mickelson would not be allowed to leave the building. These watchmen were to see to that. But they had been told, in a furtive radio message from the plane that bore Mickelson, that their guard duty wouldn't last long.

Mickelson opened his apartment door with his key, and stepped in. It spoke volumes of his ignorance of the magnitude of the game he'd unwittingly mixed in, that he reached for the light switch and clicked it on with never a thought of trouble.

Then he froze, where he was, with his arm still outstretched near the switch.

Sitting in an easy-chair, facing the door, was a man. The man had a curious little knife in his right hand.

Mickelson, with startled eyes, saw that the man's face was heavy-featured and florid. Foreign-looking. In that face were incongruously set the iciest, most deadly, most colorless eyes he had ever seen in a human countenance. They chilled his spine. They made his voice come as a sort of broken squeak when he said:

"Who . . . who are you? What are you doing here?"

Then he turned to leap back out into the hall.

The hand of the man in the chair made a light, flicking motion. The little knife he'd held glittered in flight, and embedded itself with a soft swish in the door behind Mickelson.

Embedded itself an inch from Mickelson's nose.

The chemist didn't try to run any more.

"What do you . . . want?" he whispered, after licking lips that had gone too dry to utter words without being moistened again.

"Some information," said the man with the icy, terrible eyes.

"About . . . what?"

"Where have you been since noon of yesterday?"

"Out with a fr-friend," stammered Mickelson. "I—that's all. Just out with a friend."

He felt as if his legs had turned to rubber. Felt as if all will power were draining slowly from him—drawn by the awful, colorless eyes, and the florid, absolutely immobile face.

The Avenger, still with the florid tint of Molan Brocker's face coloring his own dead-white skin, and in Molan

Brocker's clothes, stared with eyes like diamond drills. There was a shred of cotton still in Mickelson's left ear. It wouldn't have been seen by any other than Benson.

"You have just come from a plane," The Avenger said. "Evidently it was a plane built more for speed than for refined passenger service. You stuffed cotton plugs in your ears to muffle the sound of the motor. Where have you come from in that plane?"

"I . . . I wasn't in a plane!" stumbled Mickelson. "My ears are sensitive. I wear cotton plugs a lot, to keep out the roar of the city—"

"At five in the morning? There is very little roar, even in New York, at five in the morning. You came from up the coast, didn't you?"

"I don't know what you're talking about—"

But The Avenger knew he had struck home. The phrase he'd heard in the office of the Klammer Importing Co. fitted in here precisely.

"You came from up the coast. Where?"

Mickelson moistened his lips again. He couldn't get any words at all out, now. Nothing in life had ever frightened him as much as the colorless, icily flaring eyes.

The Avenger started to repeat the question, then stopped. Mickelson's right hand had gone up to loosen his collar, as if it were suddenly choking him. Benson's gaze riveted itself on the hand.

The thumb and the base of the forefinger—

His voice was a little different, as he said:

"Tell me all you know about the frosted death."

"I . . . I don't know anything about it," stammered Mickelson. "Just what I've read in the papers. I have no firsthand knowledge of it."

"I believe," The Avenger said softly, almost gently, "you have."

"No, no! I don't know a thing about it!"

Benson hesitated a moment, then made his play. It would either kill the craven thing before him with pure terror, or break him so utterly that he would tell without further stalling, whatever he knew.

He bet on the latter—and he lost.

"Oh, yes, you do," he said, in that gentle, almost sympathetic voice. "You know about the frosted death at first hand. The evidence is all too clear—*on* you!"

"What do you mean?" jerked out Mickelson.

"Look at your right thumb," The Avenger said.

Mickelson raised his right hand, stared, then glared at it with eyes so widened that you could see a ring clear around each pupil.

"Why—" he panted. "Why—"

That was his last coherent word.

On the thumb was a small patch of something that looked like powdered sugar. There was a similar, smaller patch on the first joint of his forefinger.

Mickelson glared from the white stuff, to the man before him. But his eyes didn't see that man. They saw death!

Choking, gagging, he tore the bills from his pocket, glared at them, then screaming he threw them from him. Still screaming, with white flecks on his lips, he began to batter his right hand against the wall, and to try to scrape the white stuff off.

The shock had been too much. There was stark madness in his eyes. And it was a madness that would endure the few short hours till death released him!

CHAPTER XV

Terror Walks

In a little tarpaper barn of a place, deep in the Maine woods, the tool of empire was being fashioned. Dreams of empire. One of money, to be gained by the man who was responsible for the most baffling and deadly enemy known to medical history.

The other—visions of an entire continent belonging to a nation that, at that moment, could and did raise a specter of alarm and fear in its endeavor for other lands and greater slave populations.

In that low shack, there had been twelve worktables, with only ten workers. Now there were twelve workers on the twelve tables.

The last two to be added to the robot corps were MacMurdie and Josh Newton.

They looked like the others, now. They were dull-eyed, pallid of lip. Josh's blackness had taken on a sort of leaden-gray look. They worked like automatons, filling little glass capsules with the white stuff that looked like snow, sealing each capsule, putting it aside, and starting on another.

Just two of twelve automatons, doomed to die in a few more days.

That is, they would have been if Mac hadn't left his drugstore in such a hurry the evening before.

As Mac had told Josh, when he had experimented with the white mold he had taken every precaution he could think of. Among other things, he had worn tiny, medicated pads of felt in his nostrils on the slight chance that he might inhale some of the spores.

Frequently he had replaced with new pads the ones he'd breathed through for a time. The old ones, since he had no intention of using them again, he thrust absently into the highly unsanitary depths of his coat pocket.

He hadn't bothered to take them out when he left the store yesterday.

When he and Josh had been borne into the factory, he had crawled with apprehension at the sight of all the deadly white mold around. His hands had been bound together, but not lashed to his sides, at first. So he had inserted two of the little pads in his nostrils, by a lot of contortions of his bound limbs—and two in Josh's. Even used, the pads would be a whole lot better than no nasal protection at all.

Veshnir had carefully introduced the glass tube into the nasal passages of both men and deposited some of the white death, not on the moist nasal membrane—but on the little felt pads. And when he turned and went out, the two men had simply snorted the pads out again.

Mac had put on an act, had fought furiously against Veshnir. Josh hadn't bothered to. Knowledge of the pads—and of something else—had kept him calm throughout.

The dour Scot had puzzled over that curious complacence of Josh's ever since.

"Ye look," he said now, to the long, thin Negro, "like the cat that swallowed the canary."

They had been released by one of the dull-eyed workers with the seeds of death in their brains, about two hours ago. They had found they must work at the two vacant tables. If they didn't, the other ten gathered around with clubs to force them. In their dulled brains, orders had been planted concerning Mac and Josh; and they carried out the orders like mechanical things—inexorably and without question.

The two aids of The Avenger had discovered more orders, too, when they tried to slip out the door of the little death-plant. In the first place, they had found the heavy plant door was bolted from the outside. Secondly, they had seen the ten workers charge toward them once more, to club their heads in if they didn't go back to the tables.

So they went to the tables, and they stayed at the tables. They filled glass capsules, with potential death in each for a thousand humans.

And Mac wondered audibly what made Josh so calm. They had found that they could talk all they liked. That seemed to come outside the orders left with the ten robots.

"Ye act like ye were thinkin' of maplenut sundaes—which ye'll probably never live to gorge on again," said Mac, almost resentfully.

"It's not that I'm thinking of," said Josh, with a faint smile.

"Then in Heaven's name, what is it? If ye know somethin' to smile about, share it with me."

"I am thinking," said Josh, "that every railroad track works two ways. You can go on it, or you can come on it."

Mac stared at Josh with sudden dreadful apprehension.

"I'm quite all right," said Josh, still with his faint but deadly smile. "You said there was about one chance in five that your precautions wouldn't do us any good. But apparently the chance wasn't turned against us. We'd know by now if we were going to be like the rest in here."

"Then," said the Scot, exasperated, "what's all this gibberish about railroads?"

"A railroad track runs two ways," repeated Josh. "A conduit will allow water either to go to a certain spot, or be sucked from a certain spot."

Mac snorted, and glared.

"Similarly, a glass tube will work both ways," said Josh.

"If the mold hasn't touched yer brain," growled Mac, "then the maplenut sundaes have finally gotten ye. It still has no reason in it."

"There is a chance," shrugged Josh, "that one of these unfortunates in here is not so far gone but what he can understand more than he seems—and pass it on. So that is as clearly as I will put my exceedingly pleasant thought, my friend."

So Mac simmered and stewed, wild at the realization that in his brain lay the answer to the frosted death beginning to sweep the city—and that he was held helpless here and unable to use it. And nagged also with the smaller puzzle of what the devil Josh was grinning to himself about.

In Mickelson's apartment when the doomed man's reason left him, Benson had phoned at once for a doctor. As a superb physician himself, he knew it was useless; but it seemed the least he could do.

Then he had taken off one of the raving man's shoes.

His thrust about recently coming from a plane had gone home, he knew. So the problem was to find what plane, at what airport.

Mickelson's shoe was placed on a clean sheet of paper. He scraped at the deep crease between sole and upper, and got out a tiny heap of dirt and dust.

From his pocket Benson drew something that was the only one of its kind, designed by him for just such use. It was a pocket microscope, hardly larger than a good-sized fountain pen and looking like one when it was capped. It had a tripod support that came out like three thin legs from the barrel; since no man's hand is steady enough to hold, without blurring, an instrument with a power of eight hundred diameters.

He looked at the fine debris from Mickelson's shoe and saw a curious blend of decomposed paper particles, microscopic bits of old rubber, and faint traces of iron oxide, all in the form of dust.

Newark Airport!

They were filling in at Newark, enlarging the already huge landing field. They were using the debris of the city as a fill. This stuff had come from there, telling that Mickelson had just come from Newark Airport. It was the most probable anyhow, since that was the largest field.

Benson admitted the doctor he had called, and left. He fitted the eye-cups with the gray-brown pupils over his own colorless, flaming orbs as he went down the stairs. When he stepped out of the building, he was Brocker again, from derby hat down to shoes with their special lifts.

It saved him from the men posted about the building.

One of them came quickly up to him, heavy face grim, eyes alert.

"Brocker! I did not know you were to be within the building. We were to watch outside—"

"The watch is over," said Benson, in guttural tones. "There is no more need."

"Good! We shall report—"

"It must be you that reports. I have another task. Urgent!"

He swung about with a military clicking of heels. With no more attempt at explanation—knowing, indeed, that these men did not expect to have orders explained to them—he went off.

He raced to the Newark Airport.

There, he walked slowly down the concrete run past the hangars. He went slowly—more slowly, yet, as he approached the first vast shed where private planes could rent space.

A man came out in a hurry.

"You, Brocker! What are you doing here?"

It was the tone of an executive addressing an office boy. And not a very important office boy, either.

The Avenger made his tone suitably humble.

"I have been ordered to report to you here. We go at once."

"Go where?"

"North. To the boat."

Benson knew his goal lay north, but he wasn't quite as sure of his conjecture about a submarine being involved. So he used the foreign word signifying, simply: boat, or vessel.

It developed that his caution had been unnecessary.

"Why do we go to the submarine?" snapped the man.

Some explanations were necessary, here. This man was an officer. He would telephone to confirm any order that seemed implausible.

"The man with the white hair, Benson, is heading north, it is thought. We go to warn the submarine to stay submerged, save at night, and to make sure there are no other things to give us away."

"There is the radio," said the man impatiently. "That is faster than flying."

"It is feared that Benson knows the code, and the wave length. He may overhear. That would be worse than if our submarine commander were not warned at all."

Benson looked at ease, but actually was ready to leap like the gray fox he resembled, if necessary. It was an even chance whether the man would take this in—or become suspicious.

The Avenger won, as resourceful people who seldom leave anything to chance usually do.

"Come!"

He followed the man into the hangar, to a small cabin ship whose motor roared powerfully when started. The man climbed into pilot's togs, and was revealed as the fellow who had piloted Veshnir northward.

"In!" he commanded contemptuously.

The plane took off.

Benson had been a little concerned about keeping up the pretense of being Brocker during the hours that would elapse in their flight. He needn't have been. The man at the controls was evidently so far above Molan Brocker in the military caste both belonged to, that he said not one word all the way up.

Benson reflected on the difference between these people and Americans. No two men of the United States, no matter what the gulf between them, would have maintained such a silence—stiff and arrogant on one hand, servile and slavelike on the other.

But The Avenger was using his eyes, through the make-up lenses, as well as his brain. He used them more in the advanced morning sunlight as the plane's motors cut off at twenty thousand feet.

He saw a tiny open space in thick woods as the ship glided down to land. He saw a little doll house that must be a very large log cabin. He saw a dark sliver in the water of a tiny bay nearby.

That sliver would be a submarine, submerged. From water level, all you'd see would be the top of the conning tower, open for the fresh air that is such a luxury for subs on duty. But up here you could see the entire submerged bulk.

The ship slipped into the secret landing field. It bumped to a stop. The pilot turned from the controls, and then sagged suddenly like a rag doll.

Benson sheathed Mike, the tiny .22, and stepped from the plane.

CHAPTER XVI

Flame That Failed

In the tarpaper shack where a new world war was being born, there was a huge refrigerator. It was electric, run from the log cabin's efficient electric plant. It was necessary for preserving the chopped meat with which the trays on the worktables, in which the mold was reproducing constantly, were periodically refilled.

Mac and Josh had gone regularly to the refrigerator to get more meat. Mac had hatched a plan from this.

The big white box had its motor in the bottom, and the motor was exposed by opening the bottom door, like a cupboard door. The motor was not of the newest type; it was not in a sealed case. Wiring was exposed.

About every half hour it was necessary to go to the refrigerator. That made quite a few trips. And on every trip, Mac left some of the collodion, used for sealing the little glass capsules, near the terminal of the refrigerator motor where the wires were fastened.

Collodion is pyroxilin, or guncotton, dissolved in ether.

Mac had quite a bit of the stuff in the lower compartment of the enameled white box. Even Josh hadn't noticed what he was doing, so furtively had the Scot opened the lower door a little at the times when he opened the upper, regular one, a lot.

So Mac asked him, in a slightly roundabout way:

"How would you like to burn to death?"

Josh smiled a little, lead-colored lips losing a bit of their grim straightness. The unhealthy color of his lips was produced by wiping on them dust from the floor, from time to time. This was to convince any person coming in to look things over, that Josh and Mac had indeed been made into the robots they resembled by Veshnir's manipulations with the glass tube.

"Naturally," Josh retorted, "I don't want to burn to death."

"If you could send this death factory and all the frosted death in it up in flames with you, would you risk it?"

"Certainly!" said Josh, without a moment's hesitation.

"Then rrrisk it ye shall," said the Scot, burring the r as he did when strong emotion seized him.

Josh looked puzzled.

"Next trip I make to the refrigerator," said Mac, "will start the fireworks. And I mean fireworks! We have one chance. Perhaps a section of the wood wall will burn enough, before we're roasted alive, to let us break on through to the open air."

Some of Josh's unnautral color became natural. But he nodded steadily.

Mac looked around. The ten automatons were busy at their deadly task. None paid any attention to him. Indeed, none would—unless he tried one of the two things they'd been ordered to prevent: try to get out the shack door, or try to stop working.

The Scot went to the refrigerator, opened the regular door for more chopped meat, and at the same time stealthily opened the bottom door. He slid his bony right hand in, grasped the electric cables going to the refrigerator motor.

He yanked hard.

There was blue flame as the wires pulled free and short-circuited. Following that so instantly as to seem simultaneous, there was a soft roar as the collodion ignited.

It spurted flame in a solid sheet around the motor and out the open door. Mac had leaped back, but no man could be fast enough. He gasped with the pain of singed face and hands.

The floor or rough planks was a solid sheet of fire almost before Mac could get back to Josh. And then a curious and terrible thing occurred. That was—the actions of the ten robots with the tragically deadened brains.

They couldn't think any more. Only their involuntary nervous systems were spared by the ravages of the mold. They couldn't grasp situations and act on them any more. They simply stared uneasily at the flames.

Deep instinct stirred in them. The dread of fire goes back a million years. They were vaguely afraid. But they didn't know what to do about this. There had been nothing told them, when Veshnir left, about what to do in the event of a fire.

So they stared at the rapidly growing flames, coughed in the smoke, and milled uncertainly around the tables. A few fumbled with their routine tasks. A few more went a step or two toward the door, but came obediently back. And none tried to stamp out the flames.

"Poor devils," said Mac. "They'll die like horses in a burning stable, without sense enough to try to get out into the open air."

"They're doomed anyway," said Josh gently. "And it is better like this, even if we go, too, than that these scores of thousands of little death bombs be released on European cities."

They couldn't take the heat standing up any more. They lay down—and watched the wall near the refrigerator. That section was blazing hardest. It was there that they might have the greatest chance of bursting through flame-weakened timbers.

But they were never to know whether the chance would have brought failure or success.

On the submarine, the captain had had a quite natural thought. Or, rather, a sequence of thoughts.

One was that, safe as the whole plan seemed, there was always a slight chance of something going wrong. The sub might be spotted and investigated. Something might go wrong at the building where the frosted death was being cultivated and stored in thin glass. Above all, something might go wrong in negotiations with that man, Veshnir.

A man who would see thousands of his countrymen die helplessly, for money, could not be trusted. Veshnir might receive the balance of the huge payment for his white death, and then try to refuse delivery till still more money was paid. After receiving money, he might try to stall till he could contact other European powers and sell them the white death, which would checkmate the glorious plans of the nation to which the sub captain owed allegiance.

There were many slips possible between now and the time when the completed store of glass capsules was ready to be packed on the sub.

And there was one very simple way to take insurance against some of them.

Why wait till the manufacture was completed? There were almost enough glass capsules in that little shack, now, to accomplish their plans. Why not take aboard what had been made, to date, and then just keep loading as the capsules were sealed and racked?

Then, if anything came up, the sub could dive and head for home with whatever they had on board, and all would be well. Matter of fact, it was entirely possible that he might get enough for their needs before Veshnir returned and found out what was happening. Then they could waive that final, huge payment to him, altogether.

The commander sent eight men to the tarpaper shed to bring back all the capsules ready for packing.

The eight got to the shack just as smoke began to seep from the rough cracks between planks, and spiral up in the clear morning air.

With a wild curse in his foreign, guttural tongue, the leader of the eight charged to the door, unbolted it, and rushed into the building.

If the crackle of flames hadn't been so loud, Mac and Josh might have heard the approach and continued to act like the robots they pretended to be. But they hadn't heard, were not warned, and hence were caught off base.

The leader of the squad rushed into a room in which ten men acted like dead things, with entire lack of sense in their dull eyes; and two acted like normal humans. The two were in a corner, watching the flaming wall. As clearly as if the fact had been shouted, the squad leader knew that these two were responsible for the trouble. He jumped toward them.

"Josh!" yelled Mac, knowing it was all up, "hold 'em. If we can keep 'em from getting after the fire for just a little longer—"

But that couldn't be done, either. There were too many. Eight to two!

Mac's fists, like mallets of bone, swung with a desperation that made him insensible to pain. Josh fought like a black cat. But with a machine-like precision that almost reminded them of the automatons still huddling stupidly by the worktables, the eight surrounded them and methodically cut them down.

The men from the sub stamped the fire out. Then one, with a harsh oath, drew out his service automatic and aimed it at Mac's unconscious head.

"No!"

The squad leader had a spark of imagination. Also he had a mighty fury that these two had almost wrecked the plans of his country. They deserved something worse than quick death for that.

He took one of the thousands of glass capsules in the storage racks, unhurt by the flames on the other side of the room. He came back to where the Scot and the Negro lay. The other men were grinning now.

The man dashed the glass capsule between Mac and Josh on the floor.

From it, like a genie from a magic bottle, came the almost invisible, grayish cloud of death spores. They did not hover long.

The eight men from the sub had backed as far from the capsules as they could. But they needn't have worried. The frosted death settled on the nearest victims always, and from then on could be dislodged only by contact.

The entire contents of the capsule sifted down over Josh and Mac.

"Now," said the man from the sub, "they will have a few hours to think over what they tried to do, and regret it."

On the submarine, the captain saw the spiral of smoke rising from the plant. He whirled to the speaking tube.

"All hands! To the building in the woods!"

Two men were left aboard as guards, but the rest, nineteen including the commanding officer, went hastily ashore.

The smoke wasn't spiraling upward any more. It seemed that the trouble at the death shop had been overcome. But it only confirmed the captain's thought: get aboard what capsules already were prepared, at once.

In the building, the eight were already turning to the storage racks, to lift trays of capsules. And on the floor nearby, Josh stirred a little in his unconsciousness, and moaned. But for a little while longer his senses were in an oblivion that was merciful.

Not for a little while more would they realize that in a few hours they would be like the other victims of the frosted death; that over them was forming the fine white stuff, like powdered sugar, that would turn them to snow men.

There had been no chance for quick wits, and medicated felt pads, to save them this time!

CHAPTER XVII

Two To Die

Some hours before, Mickelson had sat on one end of that rustic divan with Sangaman on the other. Now, The Avenger's gray-steel body reposed where Mickelson had been.

Before, Sangaman had sat with his head in his hands, a beaten man. Now he sat erect, chin up. And this in spite of a thing of pure horror that he had discovered a little while ago, just before this man with the awe-inspiring, colorless eyes had arrived.

That thing concerned his right hand—which he kept in his coat pocket, deep down so that even the wrist should not show.

Benson had come first to the one building he had seen from the plane: the log cabin. And there he had found this elderly man for whom all the police of all the nation were searching.

"All right," the tired fugitive had said. "You've got me. I surrender. Take me where you wish. It won't last long, for me, anyway."

"I'm not here to arrest you," said Benson. "I'm after the guilty man."

Benson had listened to Sangaman's account of all that

happened to him, with his mind clicking into place the few details he hadn't as yet known.

"Veshnir, of course," Benson snapped. I have known it since the day before yesterday, with the murder of August Taylor."

"Veshnir, of course," Benson snapped. "I have known was sure it was he, at first. Then I didn't know. Recently I have been more and more sure it wasn't. But always I was too confused to think. Why do you say the murder of August Taylor convinced you of his guilt?"

"Taylor's death releases millions in business insurance to prop up the sagging finances of the Sangaman-Veshnir Corp."

"But," said Sangaman, "since they think I did it, there will be no payment made. Insurance companies do not pay to murderers."

"Exactly," said The Avenger. "But at present they only *think* you did it. Unless they prove in court that you are the murderer, the payment must be made to the firm. And if you disappear forever, which was undoubtedly Veshnir's plan, there could never be such proof. Therefore the payment would some day be made—and greatly enrich Veshnir's company."

Sangaman shook his head.

"It would not all be his. Even with me dead, my daughter, Claudette, would get my share; so he would still own less than half. He would have to kill her, too, before it would all revert to him—"

The old man stopped, with his hands beginning to tremble. He was still keeping the right one in his pocket.

"Precisely," nodded Benson. "And the attempt to kill your daughter was made, which again nailed it all to Veshnir; only he could have profited."

"An attempt?" babbled Sangaman. "A murder attempt on my . . . on Claudette?"

"Don't worry. She wasn't hurt. And she's safe now, at my headquarters."

Benson, icy eyes glittering their pale flame, picked the story up again.

"Veshnir killed Targill in some quarrel concerning the frosted death. It does not matter what difference arose between them. It was either you or he, slated for the murder; so he framed you. Undoubtedly he slipped a drug in the thermos of black coffee you say was on your desk the night you went over the books. He went through the rigmarole of your killing Targill, in a coma from overwork, and brought you here. He killed Taylor, for the insurance millions, and left a pair of your rubber gloves from the laboratory at Taylor's house. Then he killed Mickelson because his blackmail demands threatened him as well as you—"

"Mickelson, too?" gasped Sangaman. "He is dead?"

"He's as good as dead," said Benson. "The white mold. It had almost covered his right hand when I left him. Last night Veshnir evidently managed to deposit some of the stuff on his hand. Perhaps he did it via the money Mickelson had in his pocket—"

Benson stopped. His immobile face seemed to grow more immobile, and intent, than ever. His eyes were like burnished steel as he stared at Sangaman.

"Did Veshnir touch *you* last night?" he said. "At any time? In any way?"

"No!" said Sangaman, voice level.

"Why are you keeping your right hand in your pocket? You've had it in there since I've been here."

"Just a mannerism," shrugged Sangaman. "I'm perfectly all right."

"Let me see—" Benson began.

Probably only one thing could have swerved The Avenger from his insistence on seeing that hand. That was the kind of break which occurred then, and which Sangaman noted because he was staring out a window instead of into the pale, probing eyes.

"Look!" he said. "A fire! In the woods! If that gets to the cabin—"

The Avenger was at the door before Sangaman realized he had moved. And it was not through apprehension concerning the cabin. He wasn't thinking about that.

Submarine just off this coast. Cabin here, belonging to Veshnir. Huge tract of virgin woods. It was a certainty that somewhere near here was located the death factory Benson knew must exist.

Possibly the smoke was rising from that. In any event, it was something that demanded investigation, with terrible urgency.

So he raced from the cabin, without having pressed his insistence on seeing the older man's hand. And in leaving Sangaman, he left a hero.

Sangaman was an intelligent man. He had known the dynamic power of this average-sized man with the thick white hair and the stainless-steel eyes. If anyone could solve the riddle of the frosted death, and quickly, it would be this man. Hence the less he was distracted with details the more swiftly he might deliver thousands from death.

Sangaman had refused to present The Avenger with one detail that would have been sure to distract him for at least a little while, and about which nothing could be done anyhow.

That was the appearance of the hand that Veshnir had taken in his own gloved hand some hours before.

The hand looked as if covered with powdered sugar. So did the wrist and arm it was attached to.

Sangaman's right arm looked like a snow limb almost to the shoulder.

The smoke was ceasing as Benson ran toward it. But there was still enough to guide him till his quick eyes caught the subdued black of the tarpaper building in the gloom of the woods. He got to the door of the place just as the first of the eight men inside began to come out with several trays of capsules.

And just as the crew of the submarine rushed up behind

him. There were eight men in front of him and nineteen behind.

The Avenger turned, marched up to the sub captain, and gave the stiff salute of his country.

"Molan Brocker reporting," he said. "I am of the New York organization."

He hoped fervently that none of the sub crew knew Molan Brocker. Some of the florid facial tinting was wearing off by now. And besides, there was always one cardinal danger that threatened Benson when he was disguised as another person, like this.

That was the movelessness of his paralyzed face.

But his luck was out, here.

"Brocker?" said the sub's commanding officer. "I know no Brocker."

"I have passport and credentials," said Benson.

Then one of the eight from within spoke up.

"He is Molan Brocker, as he says. Of the New York unit. I know him well."

The Avenger nodded formally to the speaker, meanwhile studying him without seeming to do so.

It was the man who had broken the capsule between Mac and Josh, though Benson did not know that. The man who had a spark more imagination and intelligence than the rest.

"Very well, Brocker, what have you to report?" the sub captain said.

"Possible danger," said Benson, playing out the part he had begun with the plane pilot, lying unconscious at the controls now. "I have been commanded to give you the message to leave your present anchorage and submerge down the coast. And you are to remain submerged during daylight hours."

The man who had said he knew Brocker was looking at Benson with a curious fixity. The Avenger didn't quite like his expression.

The sub captain's reaction was the same as the plane pilot's.

"Why did you not radio this mesage? Why was the risk taken of coming up here in person?"

"It was feared that the code and wave lengths might be known to the authorities—" began Benson.

The stare of curiosity with which the man who knew Brocker was regarding him, was becoming fixed and icy. Something was wrong! Benson could not guess what.

"You have had medical treatments in New York, Molan?" the man said suddenly.

"Medical treatments?" Benson repeated.

"Why do you not call me by my name, Molan?" the man said softly. "Surely you have not forgotten my name?"

Benson said nothing to that. Every muscle of his gray-steel body was as taut as a violin string. His brain was racing to fathom the reason for this sudden suspicion.

The crew of the sub were instinctively gathering a little closer.

"Do you remember, Molan," the man went softly on, "the time in Kolmogne when we went swimming and you saved my life?"

A trap, likely. If Benson said yes, the man was apt to say there had been no such occurrence.

"I'm afraid I do not," Benson said. "In fact, I do not remember ever having been in Kolmogne—"

"Seize him!" the man screamed. "Brocker has a twitching of his right cheek muscles. This man has not. And he does not remember our childhood in Kolmogne."

The Avenger had overestimated his man. The question had been a straight one and not a trick.

The crew leaped toward him.

The muscles of The Avenger's body seemed to have more power, pound for pound, than any normal muscle should have.

As the crew leaped toward him, he jumped straight up and forward.

His hands hooked over the edge of the tarpaper roof of the shack.

"Kill him! Our country's future is at stake!" roared the sub captain.

Pistols were whipped out with a speed indicating long hours of barrack practice. Shots were snapped with a precision hinting at days of practice on range and field. But The Avenger, with one catlike motion, had pulled himself over the edge of the roof so that he could not be seen. Half a dozen bullets struck the spot where his body had been—but no longer was.

He raced back across the roof, and jumped from the edge of it far out into space. His hands caught a tree branch. He swung again, to the crotch of a big maple.

"He's getting away through the branches! Follow him!"

The Avenger, never cooler than when danger was at its height, had Brocker's coat off. Just as the first of the men rounded the building, Benson tossed the coat.

It lit ahead, in another tree. That tree was hollow. He could see the hollow from where he was; but from the ground it did not show.

The coat struck the hollow accurately and fell into it. But the running man at the corner of the shack couldn't see that. He saw a hurtling form in the air, got a glimpse of it landing in a great tree fork, then saw it no more. And, of course, he assumed it had swung on farther into the woods.

"This way!" he yelled. "He is going this way!"

He ran forward with the rest streaming after him. All had guns in their hands now. They fired at random into the branches as they went, methodically sweeping the leafy ambush up there with searching lead fingers.

The Avenger waited till the last had gone into the woods, then calmly turned back. He lit softly on the roof of the building, walked warily so that he would not rustle the drying leaves of the branches piled there to camouflage the place from the air.

A guttural sentence indicated that not all of the men

were scattered on the false scent. At least two had been left behind.

Benson felt along the tarpaper of the roof, till he found a soft spot. Here there was a knothole in the planks under the paper. He punched through it and looked down.

For an instant he was as motionless as a block of ice. His eyes, colorless, glaring, were as terrible as drawn knives. He was looking straight down at Josh and Mac.

They were sprawled on the floor, deeply unconscious. But it was not their unconsciousness that brought that look into Benson's eyes.

Over the features of the two men was forming a whitish fine film, as if snow were sifting gently down on them as they lay.

The frosted death. It had them!

Benson faced toward the coast, leaped once more from the roof, soundlessly caught a branch, and began swinging like a gorilla toward the sea.

CHAPTER XVIII

Race Against Time

The Avenger went a quarter of a mile through the trees. It was miraculously done. No trained trapeze expert could have kept up with him. At the end of each swing, he seemed instantly to spot just the right branch, at the maximum distance ahead, and leap for it. So that his progress seemed one continuous flow of motion.

He could go faster on the ground, however; so he dropped the instant it seemed safe, and began running. He flitted through the woods like a gray streak, hurdling tree-trunks and underbrush, toward the coast.

Benson had to get to a short-wave radio transmitter. Fast! And the only one he could conceive of near here, was on the submarine.

The Avenger was acting on a theory that to him was just about accomplished fact. He knew men. In particular, he knew Mac and the rest of his aids. He was sure the dour Scot wouldn't have been captured if he hadn't left his drugstore. He was equally sure Mac would not have left his store if he hadn't found the antidote for the frosted death. The Scotchman would have kept on at his laboratory bench till he dropped from fatigue.

So there was an antidote. And Mac and Josh had been

taken with it. An antidote would be a priceless thing. So it was unlikely that it had been destroyed.

The sea was in sight, shimmering in the sun. Benson slowed his pace, stopped behind a big stump. He wasn't even breathing fast from his prodigious effort. His body, it seemed, was made of metal instead of flesh and blood.

The point at which he had emerged was at the edge of one of Maine's rock cliffs about thirty feet above the water level. Beneath, the water pounded against the rock, quite deep clear up to the foot of the cliff. Its color told that.

Out a little way was the whalelike form of the submarine, under water to the conning tower. Over the edge of the tower hatchway, showed the head and shoulders of one of the sub's crew. Left on guard. With how many others? The Avenger could not guess.

Benson's hand went down to his leg, came up with the slim, blued butt of Mike, the .22, in it.

It was a long shot. Over a hundred yards, and down. It isn't easy to shoot from an elevation. But Benson probably had no peer in marksmanship. The colorless, glacial eyes lined the sights up for about four seconds, and then he squeezed the trigger.

The man in the conning tower suddenly disappeared. There was no sound, no move. He simply slid down out of sight.

It seemed there was another man just below him. This one appeared like a jack-in-the-box, with a submachine gun poking inquisitively around over the hatch rim.

The fall of the first man must have seemed like a ghastly miracle to this man. No sound. No one near, as far as could be seen. Yet the first man had slumped down the iron rungs of the tower ladder, apparently clubbed on the top of his head!

Mike spat another leaden pea. The second man threw up

his hands and fell back within. The gun he had held splashed into the water and sank.

Benson let a minute pass. No third head showed. He holstered Mike, fastened a waterproof hood over the holster. Then he straightened on the cliff edge.

Below, the surface next to the cliff was strewn with great rocks, over which water combed white. He dived, like an arrow, down the thirty feet, gliding into the water almost without a splash, with rocks to right and left so close that they almost grazed him as he passed.

He swam to the sub, lowered himself down the conning tower, and stepped over the two unconscious guards.

His steely white fingers flew at the task of altering the sub's short-wave apparatus so that it could send to the special instrument in the Bleek Street headquarters.

"Smitty? This is Benson talking. Orders. Rush!

"Telephone Veshnir. Talk in the guttural tone and with the accent we're familiar with. Tell him that it has been decided to cut the price to be paid him in half. When he protests, tell him he will take that or nothing at all, and that he is lucky to be getting that much. Then hang up. Repeat to me."

Benson turned from the receiver, satisfied, as Smitty repeated the message.

He was betting that Veshnir had some of the antidote at all times. The man dealt with the frosted death. What more natural than that he should carry some with him, in case he was unexpectedly attacked by the mold?

Everything was being wagered on this, with the lives of Josh and Mac as the stake. Wagered on this—and on the time element.

The Avenger's pale eyes probed around. From a locker he got a collapsible rubber raft. He took it above, inflated it, and tossed it into the water. Then he dragged the two men up, laid them on it, and floated them toward shore. He went down the iron ladder one more time.

Benson opened the submersion tanks of the underseas craft, and darted back up the conning tower. Water was just beginning to slide over the rim as he got out. The submarine lurched downward, settled at a crazy angle, and sank in forty-five feet of water.

At the Sangaman-Veshnir Corp., Veshnir tilted back in his swivel chair in a pleasant mood. He had never looked more kindly, more benevolent. He coughed. He'd caught cold or something, and it was bothering his throat. But aside from this minor detail the world was perfect.

Things could not have gone better. Mickelson, by incredible luck had gone mad when he discovered what had happened to him; so that even if he wished to tell what little he knew, before death took him, now he would be unable to do so. Soon Sangaman would be out of it, a victim of his own plotting, as far as the world knew.

He had a million. Vast additional sums were to come for the frosted death and later, for the antidote. There were Taylor's millions to be paid into the coffers of the company when it was found that the insurance people would never be able to prove their claim against Sangaman. The company would be all his when he tended to Claudette Sangaman.

That had been Veshnir's sole defeat so far. He hadn't eliminated the girl who was to inherit her father's share of the business. Eventually, he would. But for the moment that was the sole fly in the ointment—

Fate proceeded to hand him another one. For it was right then that his phone rang, and a guttural voice insolently informed him that the purchase price for the white death was to be cut in half and if he didn't like it he knew what he could do about it.

Up in the north woods a man with icy, inhuman eyes and a brain that burned with the flame of genius, had pulled the wires of psychology. This man knew how to play on the basic emotions—fear, greed, hate. He had chosen greed as the organ stop, this time, and down here, several hundred miles away, the man named Veshnir danced to the music—exactly as The Avenger had foreseen.

When the phone clicked off, shutting from his ears the

harsh, guttural insolence of that voice, Veshnir leaped to his feet. All his plans were crashing. It was incredible, but they were. And in his skull one big question mark burned and seared.

Why?

The arrangement had been concluded to everyone's satisfaction. The price had been agreed on with no quibble at all. Now the country he had dealt with was welshing.

Why?

What had occurred to make that country think it could treat him like this? What had made them feel independent of him?

Veshnir was running while the thoughts coursed through his brain. For he knew the answers at once.

Fool that he was, he had come down here to New York, leaving his little factory in the woods unguarded. He had not dared to hire guards; he had felt he'd better be on deck in the city most of the time for an alibi. And he had taken a chance on leaving his plant alone, with a submarine full of men nearby.

They had stolen the capsules already made. That's what they had done. It was probably all they really needed. Now, with what they wanted already theirs, they could slash the price on the balance! Perhaps they'd refuse *all* payment.

Veshnir was in his limousine now. The chauffeur, at the snapped order, raced down Fifth Avenue with the tires screaming under the acceleration.

They were double-crossing him! They were trying to gouge him out of some of his millions! But he'd stop that when he got up there. He had a weapon in reserve. The antidote.

The men from the sub would either bring back to the plant all the capsules they had taken and promise to go on with the payment, or he would release the antidote at once, in New York and to any European country who wanted it! That would show them!

Veshnir got to the airport in eighteen minutes. In another six he was up in the fastest plane available, with his own hands on the controls. He was not a very expert pilot; one of the many wealthy amateurs who could just barely handle a ship and that was all. But he was good enough to get about two hundred and sixty miles an hour out of the roaring motor as it headed for Maine.

It had all worked out as the man up in the north woods had planned—like a master's chess game. But the man with the icy, colorless eyes, who had so deftly pulled the strings of psychology, was still sitting on a powder keg that might blow up under him at any moment.

He had sunk the sub. No wholesale death would cross the Atlantic in *that* vessel, at least.

But surrounding the death factory that was still the vital point of the whole game, and in which Mac and Josh lay dying, were almost the entire crew of the submarine, in full possession. Close to thirty of them, all skilled at fighting and military tactics, all picked men on a mission for which any one of them would fanatically give his life.

CHAPTER XIX

Death Plant

Fergus MacMurdie was not only brave in the face of death, but also he was resigned to it as a man would naturally be who has no human ties to make him want to live. The Scot had always known he'd die with his boots on if he fought crime under The Avenger. But he hadn't cared. The loss of his wife and the little boy in the racket explosion some time before had made him indifferent to fate.

Now, when he slowly came to in the tarpaper building, and looked down to see his bound hands taking on the appearance of powdered sugar, he wasn't too frantic. He was somberly desperate at the thought that he, alone, had in his head the secret of an antidote that would save New York—and that he was going to die with that knowledge unused. But there was little personal emotion involved.

Josh, next to him, had more to live for. He had his pretty wife, Rosabel, who adored him and whom he adored. He had a good life under Benson, whom he looked on as superhuman.

Josh wasn't nearly as resigned as Mac. But the Negro was a brave man, too. There was no complaining.

"Whoosh!" said Mac. "I itch all over. And I feel like

a cold blanket was slowly pressin' tighter and tighter around me."

"It feels more like a warm blanket to me," said Josh quite calmly.

"That's right—argue me to death, at a time like this!"

The pessimistic Scot was a curious person. When things were going smoothly, he was the gloomiest soul alive. When everything was against him, and he couldn't conceive of a possible way out, he was the soul of optimism.

"You've experimented with this stuff," said Josh. "You know something about it. How long will it be before we sink into a coma—and don't come out again?"

Mac craned to see his hands. They were the only part of him he could see, so tightly was he bound. He estimated the stage of advancement.

"About half an hour, maybe three quarters," he said.

"It looks for once as though the chief were licked, doesn't it?" reflected Josh.

"Mon," said Mac, shocked even at such a moment, "how can ye burble such a thing? No livin' mon will ever lick the chief!"

"But a whole military corps, from a warlike, military nation?" said Josh. "What can even the chief do against a force like that?"

"Ye'll see," said Mac. "Though," he added "ye may have to see it from a pearly cloud, instead of from on earth. Unless it happens awful fast—"

The door of the plant was thrust open.

The submarine crew, with the bleak efficiency of their tribe, had combed the woods around the shack for miles in every direction. They had searched till it would seem no rabbit could escape their dragnet. In the search, they had come upon the log cabin belonging to Veshnir. Naturally, they had searched that, too. And in it had been Sangaman.

The sub captain was puzzled. Veshnir had mentioned the existence of the cabin, but he had said nothing about a tenant. The captain didn't know whether Sangaman was dangerous or not. But he took no chances.

He tied the old man's hands behind him, lashed his arms to his sides, and marched him at pistol point to the shack in the woods.

In the process, he noticed a little too late that Sangaman's right arm, to an unguessable point up under his sleeve, was whitened with the deadly mold. But he was pretty sure he hadn't touched the stuff in binding Sangaman.

It was to shove the old man roughly into the building that the door had been opened, as Mac and Josh had observed. They bound Sangaman's legs, then, and propped him against the wall in a sitting position, next to the other two.

Sangaman stared at the whitening features of Mac and Josh.

"Good heavens!"

"Ye're right with us, in more ways than one, it seems," said Mac, who had seen the frosted hand.

"Yes. I— Oh, my heavens!"

Sangaman had taken in his surroundings, then. The rack on rack of deadly glass capsules. The ten automatons, back at their work, filling the tiny containers while, slowly, they died on their feet.

"So *this* is the final answer to all Veshnir's doings," Sangaman said hoarsely. "We'll pray that *he* can do something."

"He?" repeated Josh sharply.

"Richard Benson," said Sangaman.

Mac writhed convulsively in his bonds, though the smothering white blanket had weakened him a lot.

"The chief!" he grated. "Here! What did I tell you, Josh?"

"Nothing he can do to save us," sighed Josh.

"Maybe he can't do anything for *us*. But he'll beat this frosted death before he's done. We'll see—"

There was the tramp of feet outside. The door opened. The commanding officer of the submarine came in.

The man was a maniac. His face was white with fury. His eyes had a glaze to them, like the eyes of a mad lynx. He tried twice before he could speak. Then, it was in his own tongue. English was utterly beyond him at the moment.

"My boat has been scuttled!" he raved. "Sunk in the harbor! My fine boat! Do you know anything about that, any of the three of you? *Do* you?"

Mac didn't know the language used. But Josh, honor graduate of Tuskegee Institute, had a working knowledge of it.

He translated to Mac, voice vibrant with triumph.

"The sub's sunk, Mac. This gang's marooned here. Now, who do you suppose would have done such a thing?"

"I wonder," said the Scot, frosted lips grinning.

The sub captain screamed in rage. He kicked Josh.

"Speak up! Answer! Do you know anything about this? Are more of your men around here? Was it the man who said he was Brocker? Tell me! I want that man. I'll cut him to pieces with my own hands."

Josh said nothing. In the first place, he had nothing to say, since he knew no more about it than the frenzied captain. In the second place, he wouldn't have talked if he *had* known.

The officer pulled out a knife. His voice sank to cold calmness which was more menacing than shouts.

"Speak," he said, "or I'll cut *you* to bits first!"

Josh stared up at him, calmly, a man as good as dead anyhow.

The knife went down toward his ear.

"I wouldn't!" came a quiet but compelling voice.

It had the effect of a bomb explosion.

The voice had come from above. Everyone stared up at the ceiling.

Up there, a hole about the size of a silver dollar showed where the tarpaper had been punched out above a knothole.

Through this could be seen an eye. It was pale, inhuman, as cold as ice under moonlight. It seemed to transfix the sub captain like a bayonet, and hold him motionless for a moment. But only for a moment.

He yelled out a curse, and dove for his gun!

The icily flaring eye was suddenly staring at the man over a small, blued barrel. The captain, to whom no gun smaller than a battleship's cannon had much meaning, pulled out his gun. A little thing like that might give him a flesh wound in the shoulder, or a small hole in the arm, but that would be all—

Mike lisped out a silenced bullet, and the captain went down. Slanting down the back and top of his skull, was a gash where the slug had creased him.

He fell just as two men came in with trays of the capsules in their arms. They had taken them to the shore, found no boat to put them in and had brought them back, not knowing what else to do with the things.

They had barely presence of mind enough to set them on a table instead of just dropping them, before they charged out again and began climbing to the roof, through which had come the shot.

That was all right with Benson. One or two at a time, he could handle this mob of foreign fanatics. He waited till a head showed over the roof edge, and fired again. The man clumped to the ground.

The second man didn't make the same mistake. He put his gun hand alone over the roof edge, and began firing blindly but methodically, slowly fanning the roof with bullets.

Mike equally methodically spat a neat, small bullet that shattered the wrist that barely showed. The man yelled and dropped back beside his unconscious companion.

However, that was the end of that kind of fighting. The whole crew came, drawn by the commotion and the sound of the second man's shots.

At all times, The Avenger carried around his taut waist the thin but marvelously strong silk cable, attached to the little collapsible grappling hook, which enabled him to climb things you wouldn't dream anything but a fly could ascend.

The hook was embedded in the fork of a great tree, thirty feet from the ground. The cable trailed from it to the roof.

With the approach of the other men, Benson grasped the thin cord, shoved powerfully out from the roof, and sailed off in a great arc in which he almost touched the ground at the center, and landed in another tree many yards away at the end of the swing. The men streamed after him. This time they would get this wilderness will-o'-the-wisp!

Benson had carefully swung to the north. This was because the secret landing field was to the south of the death factory.

He crashed north through the tree-tops for three or four minutes, with the men following him easily because of the noise he made. They were insane with rage. Several tried to swing up into the branches and follow in the same manner in which Benson fled.

The results were rather unfortunate. No man there could travel that way. So they picked themselves up off the ground and trailed along on foot again.

But then, abruptly, there wasn't any more crashing noise to follow. The woods were as still as the tomb.

"Here! He stopped here, in this big fir!" one of the men called. He had been nearest the sounds when they stopped.

They ringed the tree. There was enough of a clear space around it to see if anyone swung to the next tree. And they saw that no one did. They shot up into it for a while, and then several started cautiously to climb it.

Benson watched them for a few seconds from two hundred yards to the south, then swung silently on. Toward the landing field. He had left the big fir well before the first of his pursuers had got there.

The Avenger's amazingly keen ears had caught something that wouldn't be audible to the rest for another minute or two. That was the sound of an airplane motor.

Whatever plane was propelled was being catapulted at top speed. The motor in the far distance sounded like the buzz of an enraged wasp. Benson's eyes glinted. He increased the pace of his aerial journey, passing swiftly through trees bare of leaves, catching his poise again in the shelter of evergreens.

By now the noise of the plane was quite loud. Over it Benson could hear the men yelling far in the distance as they heard it also. At least half of them would race to investigate it too. But, Benson thought, at the speed at which the ship was settling, he would get to the pilot before any of them did.

He increased his pace, swinging onto the edge of the field just as the plane's wheels touched.

It made a bumpy, inexpert landing. It had scarcely stopped rolling when a man jumped out. And the man was Veshnir.

Benson had slipped over his colorless eyes the eye-lenses with the gray-brown pupils on them. He hadn't Molan Brocker's overcoat any more; he had tossed it into the hollow tree. Brocker's derby had long since gone. But over his thick white hair The Avenger still had the wig simulating Brocker's closely-cropped hair, and the lifts were still in his shoes. Once more he would take the place of the man who was held prisoner at the moment at Bleek Street.

He marched up to Veshnir, shoulders rigidly erect, walking in a heavy-footed, military fashion.

Veshnir grabbed him by the shoulder, coughing.

"You—" he sputtered, with the promised loss of millions of dollars in his mind. "You—Where is your superior officer?"

Benson's "superior officer" wasn't in circulation. But a lot of his men were going to be here in about two minutes.

He said swiftly, in guttural, accented English:

"There has been a plot. Some of our organization wanted to keep half the payment due you, for themselves, and pretended that our government was responsible. The rest of us feared our whole glorious military plan might suffer, and we refused to agree with them. There was a fight. They won. I, alone, got away, without hat or coat. Come with me. Hide before they catch us. There! You hear? They are nearing the field even now! Hurry!"

"I'll cable your government," raved Veshnir. "I'll tell the whole thing. They'll behead your fine friends who try to cheat an honest man out of his money."

He was running as he spat this out, however. Running toward the coast, and then veering north and toward the tarpaper shack, in a wide circle around the men.

The submarine crew were split two ways. About a third of them were still ringing the great fir tree in which the sounds of Benson's retreat had last been heard. It was a big tree and took a lot of searching if you wanted to be methodical about it. And it was a characteristic of these men's training that they were extremely methodical.

All the others were investigating the unexpected arrival of the fast plane, fanning out around the field to try to locate whoever had come in it.

Around the little factory there was no one at all.

Benson urged Veshnir in. The first thing Veshnir saw was the sub captain, unconscious on the floor.

"He was one who fought against the plot?" he began. Then he stopped. A fit of coughing racked him.

Mac and Josh and Sangaman, bound, were glaring up at him—with Mac and Josh hardly conscious any more. And the marks of fire scarred the wall near the refrigerator, while the racked, completed capsules were all disarranged.

"What's been going on here?" demanded Veshnir. "Why is Sangaman here? What—"

He stopped. A knifepoint like a needle had touched his throat. Then the edge of the blade, razor-sharp, settled with steady menace against his jugular.

"The antidote, please, Veshnir," Benson said, abandoning Brocker's guttural accent.

"Why—What in the world—I don't know what you're talking about. What antidote?"

Benson's hands were going over Veshnir, however; and

they paused at a lower vest pocket. The Avenger drew out a slim glass vial, tightly stoppered, filled with a bluish-green substance.

He stared at Mac. The Scotchman could hardly see, and he couldn't talk at all; but he made out the color of the vial; and his lips moved.

"Yes," was the word they formed.

There were tremendous stakes involved in this great game of the frosted death. But Benson's first allegiance was to his aids. That was the way The Avenger always worked.

"Untie Sangaman," he said to Veshnir.

Veshnir fumbled with the knots.

"Faster!"

Veshnir completed his task in a hurry. Meanwhile, Benson reached behind him and fastened the door. There was an inner, as well as an outer, bolt.

"Mac, does this antidote go through clothing the same as the mold it attacks?"

Again Mac managed to form the word: "Yes," with his numbing lips.

"Sangaman, take this vial. Shake some of the stuff in it over these two men. Save some for yourself and put it on your arm. I don't know whether it will act fast enough—"

But the profound relief in Mac's dimming eyes answered Benson. The Scot knew that it *would* act fast enough to save them, and his eyes showed it. The tensity of The Avenger's flaming, terrible orbs ceased somewhat.

Veshnir was coughing again. And Josh was staring at him with a very curious look in his eyes. A look that was calm, grim, knowing, inexorable—the way a judge might look at a prisoner being led to the gallows.

"Cut them loose, please, Sangaman," Benson said.

Sangaman slashed Mac's and Josh's bonds. Benson nodded and then suddenly whirled.

The sub commander had regained consciousness, and cunningly concealed it till he had a little strength back. Then he had leaped from the floor, like a crouching cat, at

The Avenger's back. But The Avenger had heard the light rasp of his shoe just in time.

He braced to the charge of the man, and battered him down with one lightning blow to the throat. But the action took just long enough for Veshnir to escape.

Moving faster, under the stimulus of fear and greed, than anyone ever would have thought he could move, he got to the door, and tore the bolt back.

"Everybody! Here!" Benson heard him shouting, as he leaped outside.

The Avenger raced after him, but he was too late!

The sub's crew had returned from the big fir tree where, to the last, they'd thought Benson was hiding; and from the landing field where Veshnir had just set his plane down.

They swarmed around Veshnir and Benson. The Avenger's hand darted out to close the door again and bolt it from the inside, but a crashing boot was fast enough to prevent that.

The commander of the sub came unsteadily up behind Benson, shoved him savagely aside and strode out among his men.

"Well? Well?" he snapped. "Reports! What has happened?"

One of them spoke up. One who had just come from the landing field.

"We found two planes on the field. One has been here for some time. It is the plane that has been here before. At the controls is divisional commander Buehlow, unconscious. The motor is cool; so that plane has been here for some time. The other plane is empty. The hot motor shows that it has just landed a few—"

"I came in that," said Veshnir. He was glaring at The Avenger in grim triumph. "I got here just in time, it seems."

"How it is that you came at all?" the sub captain growled at him.

"There was a phone message to me in New York leading me to believe that your nation was thinking of trying to cut the final payment to me for the frosted death—"

"What?" howled the officer, glaring at Veshnir. "You dare to think my nation would do such a thing? It is an insult!"

His voice was all the louder for the very fact that he, personally, had had just those thoughts in mind when he gave orders to load on the sub whatever capsules were already completed.

Veshnir cringed.

"It was a plot, of course. I should have known."

The captain was pacing back and forth in front of the tarpaper shack. The men ringed Benson and Veshnir stolidly but watchfully.

"So!" the captain said. "These men up here know of our plans! At least one man in New York—the one who alarmed you into coming here—knows of them. We must act fast."

"I would suggest," ventured Veshnir, "that you load the submarine—"

"We have no submarine," cut in the captain, looking murderously at Benson. "But—there are two planes on the landing field. Buehlow's is the largest?"

"Yes," said Veshnir. "It's a twelve-passenger job." His body suddenly shook with coughs.

The captain looked a little puzzled by the violence of the attack. So did Veshnir—a little worried. However, the captain had plans more important than the fact that Veshnir seemed suddenly to be catching a hard cold.

"You!" he snapped to one of the men. "Go with ten of the men to the large plane. You are a good pilot. Refuel with whatever petrol there is in the smaller ship—"

"No, no!" bleated Veshnir. "That will leave me stranded here!"

"Not for long," the captain reassured him. He turned back to the man. "Go to New York. Report at headquarters there. Get a big transport plane and return. The rest of us will leave here in that, taking the glass capsules with us. We can carry them to whatever ship of ours is closest on the Atlantic."

The eleven men started off.

"Wait," said the captain. "One more thing. While you are draining the tanks of the small plane into the larger, one of you return with five gallons of the petrol—here."

Veshnir stared quickly at the man.

"We leave no tracks," the captain explained. "We shall burn this shed where the capsules have been filled."

Veshnir nodded swiftly.

"Of course! Just the thing to do. And we'll lock this man, Benson, and all the others, in it when we set fire—"

"No," contradicted the captain, "we will not. See, now: the fire may be reported, and people come to investigate. If nothing is found but charred embers, they think only a trapper's shack or some empty storage shed has burned. They think nothing of it, and go away. But if they find the skeletons of a dozen men—immediately there is much commotion, much search. And searchers *might* pick up our trail in time to stop us before we can get offshore."

Two of his men went into the shed. They began roughly bundling the occupants out—Mac and Josh having to be carried.

A man came from the landing field with a can of gasoline. On order, he poured it over the shed floor, and the walls and worktables. The volatile, high-test stuff soaked into the dry wood.

All this time The Avenger was standing quietly, acting like a defeated man. Which, had his enemies known it, was the time when he was most dangerous of all.

Benson was watching with hawk eyes everything that went on.

"But the capsules!" said Veshnir.

"We shall take those to the cabin," said the captain. "Or, better yet, direct to the landing field. There we will await the transport—"

From the field came the sudden roar of a motor. The plane which Buehlow had piloted down here, was taking off. They watched it soar up over the trees, and head south to the big city.

"They will be back soon," said the captain. "It is well. Success is ours, after all."

"And these men?" said Veshnir, nodding toward Mac and Josh, Sangaman and Benson and the ten robot workmen.

"We shall take them to the plane, bound. And one by one we shall drop them in the sea, far out." The commander turned to the crew left with him.

"Into the shed. Get the racks of capsules and bear them to the landing f—*Stop that man!*"

Studying each event as it came up! Turning it over in his mind! Never admitting defeat! Always there was a possibility of twisting situations to an enemy's ruin, even if no other man might have discerned it—

And The Avenger had found the right combination of circumstances here. Had found it—and acted on it.

Without a ripple of warning, or the difference of an eye blink, he had leaped straight backward toward the shed. He was through the door, had it slammed, and was bolting it when the first vicious shots began to rip through the panel.

He threw himself to the floor while the slugs sang over him.

The pale eye glittered with that light which so many master crooks had seen with terror. He was alone in this building, with potential death for unknown thousands of human beings neatly racked along one wall.

And the building had been made into an almost explosive fire trap by the aviation gasoline.

Once flame had roared and crackled here, almost to ruin plans of empire. They should do so again, and this time they should not fail.

The Avenger's friends often insisted that the gray-steel man was a walking laboratory. From special pockets all over his garments, they said, he could haul enough chemicals and apparatus to start a government lab. This was a little exaggerated. But Benson did always have with him a few shells of commoner chemicals which, he had found by experience, often came in handy.

One of these was thermit, the fire-producing chemical. His steel-strong fingers dipped into a special inner pocket of his vest, worn under Molan Brocker's clothes. They came out with all the little thermit shells he had. Five. He threw them with all his strength at five different parts of the room!

The place actually seemed to explode, with such violence did the five fires start. And in the center of the swift volcano was The Avenger. Shots told him he couldn't get out through the door. But in his icily flaring eyes was no agitation. It was well worth the death of any man, to destroy the brew in this dread place.

Outside, the sub commander had got over his first maniacal fury. His rage was colossal, but now a little under control. Veshnir, however, wasn't controlled.

"Stop the fire!" he screamed. "Stop it, I tell you! Stop it! *Stop* it!—"

He doubled over in a convulsion of coughing. And Mac, lying on the ground but rapidly getting better as his parasite antidote swiftly devoured the white mold on his body, stared with wide eyes at Josh—who nodded.

Mac had seen something that Veshnir was just beginning to see. Something on Veshnir's hand, held to his lips as he coughed and strangled.

Something from his throat, like particles of wet snow, or white moss.

"Another defeat!" snarled the sub commander, voice thick. "But we are *still* not beaten. You, Veshnir, have the secret of the white death in your brain. We shall simply make more—"

Veshnir hadn't even heard. He was staring at his hand. His lips were moving, but no sound came out.

"I see," Mac said softly to Josh, "what ye meant when ye said *a glass tube works both ways.*"

Josh nodded again.

"He put that glass tube up our nostrils, and blew, to make us like the other robot workmen. But he didn't seem to think of the very simple fact that it could work both ways. When he got to me, before he could blow, I breathed down myself, a little. And what I was hoping for, has happened. A very little of the frosted death got either in his throat or lungs. And now—"

Veshnir's wild scream cut off all other sounds. It ripped at last from his palsied lips.

"I've got it too!" he screamed. "The white death! Antidote! I must get some of the antidote! This plane—New York—My laboratory safe—"

But there was no plane. The larger of the two had taken off minutes ago—leaving the smaller with a dry tank. Veshnir was marooned here for hours; and he would not last that long. The terrible knowledge gleamed insanely in his eyes—along with a last, impossible hope.

"The vial!" he screamed. "The vial that devil robbed me of and used on *these* three! There may be a little in the bottom! There may be—"

Richard Henry Benson, the Avenger, followed an inflexible practice with super-criminals. He did not want to turn them over to the regular courts, where with smart lawyers they might delay justice endlessly or even evade it in the end. And he did not want to kill them with his own hand.

Therefore, out of the flaming genius of his mind, it was his habit to maneuver them into situations where they should destroy themselves by acting on their own greedy, murderous instincts.

This time, The Avenger was directly responsible. Fate, and the quick wits of one of Veshnir's victims, had done the maneuvering. But the result was just as implacable.

Screaming, Veshnir dashed toward the flaming building. He began to batter at the door, heedless of searing hands and face.

The door went down, weakened by the fire. Veshnir, no longer a rational being, still screaming, leaped over it into a furnace. He went down on hands and knees, and scrabbled in the flame for the one thing on earth that might possibly save him. The vial in which there still might be a little of the antidote—

The roof came down! He was seen and heard no more!

Outside the inferno, the sub commander stared at Mac and Josh and Sangaman. His hand went for his gun. But only rested on the butt. He was drained—crushed—as any fanatic is when the thing he lives for has been taken away. He only stood there, shoulders drooping, legs wide apart as if barely able to support his sagging weight.

And then his hand left his gun.

"Of what use to kill these three?" he mumbled thickly. "The thing is done, now. It means nothing. Nothing at all has meaning."

He stood that way, staring emptily at the three men who were recovering from the white death, for a long time. For so long a time that one of the crew coughed diffidently, to remind him that there were orders to be given.

The foreign naval officer straightened a little.

"We shall not stay here needlessly. The fire may draw someone. March south, down the coast, to the first town. We shall radio New York from there, and have the transport pick us up—Though I think that suicide may be the better move for me in the end."

They filed off through the woods without a backward glance, each pair of shoulders bowed as though with a crushing load. Though their only burden was shattered dreams of swift, vast conquest.

And The Avenger came from behind a nearby tree, in his swift, noiseless glide. As he came, he sheathed Mike. Had the captain gone ahead and drawn that gun, Benson would have been forced to break his rule and kill.

"Chief!" whispered Mac, sitting up a little. "We thought —How on earth did ye—"

The Avenger's dead face turned toward the blazing embers which was all that was left of the shed.

"There was a refrigerator in there," he said. "It was big enough, with the trays out, to hold my body. Refrigerators, of course, are insulated. Fronted against the rear wall with the open door, it protected me like an insulated white shell till I could cut through with Ike."

He patted the special-steel throwing knife at his left calf. But words and move were absent, empty.

The fire lit up his wax-dead face and white hair. Fire that was saving nations from immediate war. The Avenger had succeeded in the greatest venture yet. But as always, success brought no content to his pale and awful eyes. He did not work for content. He knew that was impossible. He worked only to avenge the memory of his wife and daughter, killed by such scum as these—and for whose deaths all other scum should pay.